THE TALKING BOARD

The Scientific Investigations of Marianne Starr
Book Two

ISSY BROOKE

LONDON, 1890

One

Inspector Gladstone compulsively straightened everything on his desk as he spoke in measured tones, his working-class origins still shading his words with the grubbiness of the streets. But he was in charge of this London police station now, with an office of his own and everything a man of authority would need, on display all around him. Polished wood, and shiny brass, were the themes. He addressed the middle-aged constable, Bolton, but he was looking directly at Marianne while he spoke.

"You must treat Miss Starr exactly as if she were a man, Bolton."

"Yes, sir."

She smiled to herself.

"I do mean what I say," Inspector Gladstone insisted. "She is a professional, in her field. She has been educated. I have, insofar as is possible, set her expertise quite above yours. At least, in scientific matters. You can only overrule her in questions of policing. Do you see?"

"Yes, sir. Happy to, sir."

Fat Constable Bolton seemed disinclined to argue. He

smiled and nodded, and looked remarkably at ease. Inspector Gladstone seemed worried about that, and so was Marianne, now that she thought about it.

"Well, then," Inspector Gladstone said, nudging the stack of yellow paper one eighth of an inch to the left, and then nudging it back to its original position. "Well. Tonight, you shall have the full run of Rosedene and let us meet again tomorrow evening, where you can tell me all about the screaming."

The screaming, as it turned out, was not what she had expected.

***

Constable Bolton continued to be strangely affable as he walked with Marianne from the railway station to Rosedene. They were still technically in London, but it didn't feel familiar. The area was old, with large rambling houses set in private grounds all walled and hedged about. Already, progress was nibbling at the edges of the suburb, as the city expanded and brought progress, development and demolition with it, flattening the old houses to put long terraces in their places. Rosedene itself was far enough away from that to be as yet untouched.

"The Inspector is such a worrywart," Bolton said in a chatty manner. He walked slowly so that Marianne could keep up, her skirts tangling her legs as she swished through fallen leaves on the pavement. "But me, see, I know how the world works."

So did Gladstone, Marianne thought. He was a rough young man, who had worked his way through the ranks, coming up from the streets like so many of the emerging influencers did. Such backgrounds made them effective – and something to be feared, too, by the upper classes, who did not understand why justice could not continue to be forced down on the masses from above.

She didn't say anything. Bolton prattled on. "I'm quite happy to let a woman be in charge. My mother was in charge. My wife is now in charge. My daughter, well, what she says, goes, in our house. Ha. Ha." He laughed like a donkey and Marianne felt embarrassed in case someone heard him and looked their way. Maybe people would think she was being arrested, and that thought amused her, though it should not have done. "So you go ahead and be in charge, my lovely, and I shall do whatever you tell me! Ha. Ha. Ha."

"Thank you," she said politely. "I have no intention of becoming a drill sergeant and ordering you about. We are there to simply observe this reported strange phenomena. Have you a fear of ghosts at all, Constable Bolton?"

"Don't believe in them, miss. Not for one second. Life is odd enough without having things what are not alive running around as well."

"You are very sensible. Ah! The brass plate says Rosedene. We are here."

They both stood still for a moment and gazed through the twisted, rusty metal gates, which must stand permanently open. The path curved around, with lumpen cypresses along its edges, and the house itself was completely hidden from the road.

"It is very much the place for a little Gothic adventure,"

Marianne said. "I expect it to be all covered in ivy, with darkened windows and carved wood quite everywhere."

They crunched up the mossy gravel and came face to face with the house. Bolton laughed again. "You were right, miss. If I had to live here, I'd be screaming too. We shall find a hysterical kitchen maid at the root of all this, don't you think?"

"I quite agree."

They rang the bell.

And waited for far too long before it was answered.

***

It was September and dusk fell early. The darkness came even earlier to Rosedene. In the true manner of Gothic houses, most of it was shut up, and only a few rooms were lived in by the odd bundle of occupants. The house was older than Marianne had first thought, with the huge central hall having an almost medieval feeling to it, due to its size and exposed timber beams. There was a wide cold fireplace with a pile of dry pinecones in the grate, and shadowy portraits leered at them from the dark walls. Mrs Peck, the housekeeper, left them by the fireplace and went off in search of Mrs Newman. "She's not really American," the housekeeper had said cryptically, in an apologetic tone before she left.

Bolton and Marianne looked at one another in surprise. The policeman's mouth twitched in a smile, and he said in a low voice, "That's the one who's called us here, this Mrs Newman."

"I glanced at the information the Inspector had put

together. I know she's a widow, just returned here – from America, obviously, but she's actually English – and she thinks there is something strange going on." Marianne looked around. "She's probably just allergic to dust and darkness and spiders. I can't blame her."

She was expecting a widow to match these dark surroundings, all shambling and cobwebbed, with a hint of opium in the air about her. She was disappointed. Mrs Newman walked stiffly into the hall, her boots clicking on the floor, with a determined and most proprietorial march. Oddly proprietorial, given that this was not her house. She was tall, willowy and elegant, with a restrained glamour in her choice of clothing. She had lost her husband over a year ago and so appeared to be somewhere between second mourning and ordinary mourning. Everything was black, of course, but she wasn't totally submerged in crape and Marianne thought her dress had a shine to it, suggesting silk rather than light-absorbing bombazine. But then, who did follow the rules to the letter, these days? Her pale skin was heavily powdered and seemed almost floury around the edges. She smiled in a way that did not make lines on her face, and shook Marianne's hand first, very firmly indeed, and then greeted Constable Bolton.

When she spoke, she had a gravelly edge to her voice. Not quite American, but certainly not the pinched accent of the well-to-do English. "Thank you both so much for coming. I confess, Miss Starr, I am baffled and intrigued as to the source of these night-time howlings, and I am dreadfully afraid of the effect it may be having on my good aunt. She is not a strong

11

woman."

"Your aunt?" Marianne said, remembering the file of scant information she'd read. "Forgive me; I thought that…"

"Oh, yes, yes," said Mrs Newman, waving her hand. A jet ring glittered. "Miss Dorothea Newman is my poor late husband's aunt, not my own, but I must tell you, she is as dear to me as she ever was to him. She is confined to her room upstairs. We all call her Miss Dorothea; she is a most marvellous woman in spite of her infirmities. The Grand Bedroom is her whole world, these days." She sighed heavily. "And that, I am afraid, is the scene of the mischief."

"Will you tell us what is going on?"

"No," she said, decisively.

Marianne was startled by her bluntness. Bolton inhaled sharply, some mixture of shock or amusement.

"You must approach the thing with open minds," Mrs Newman continued. "I know that the mind is a pliable thing and I have no desire to plant anything which might be misleading. No, I shall install you both in the room next to the Grand Bedroom. There is a connecting door. Then, if this … whatever it is … manifests itself, you may experience it for yourselves."

"What do you think it is?" Marianne asked.

"Again, I shall not let my judgements colour your thoughts. Let us discuss it over breakfast. Now, if you care to follow me, I shall lead you to the room and see that you are both made quite comfortable."

Marianne had expected to be grilled by Mrs Newman as to her qualifications and experience. Mrs Newman had approached the police, saying that there was foul play afoot in her house, and it was Inspector Gladstone who had suggested they call in "Miss Starr, the investigator of the paranormal." The Inspector had told Marianne that Mrs Newman agreed immediately. She had seemed very pleased, in fact, that Marianne was to be brought in, and that in itself made Marianne wonder what was going on.

They were led up the wide stairs that took them to the first floor of the west wing, the only inhabited part of the building. The corridors were wide and lined with tables and chairs, all covered in dust sheets. The Grand Bedroom was at the far end, but they were not taken in to meet the older Miss Newman, the elderly Aunt Dorothea. Instead, Mrs Newman took them both into the smaller room to the side of the Grand Bedroom. She gestured at the open door but dropped her voice. "My aunt sleeps for most of the time," she said. "And she sleeps more in the daytime, for during the night she is disturbed by the noise."

"Why does she not move bedrooms?" Marianne asked.

Mrs Newman flicked her eyes to the heavens for a moment, as if asking for strength. "Exactly," she said in a tired voice. "Something that I myself have been urging her to consider. But you know how the older generation can be. There is a stubbornness born of such determination to simply survive. Now, I shall have Mrs Peck bring you food and drink. Is there anything more than you may need?"

"This is sufficient," Marianne said.

Mrs Newman left. Marianne immediately crept to the second open door and peered into the spinster aunt's bedroom.

It was gloomy. There was no light getting past the heavy

curtains at the windows, no hint of a streetlight or visible slither of moon. The only illumination came from a candle that was only an inch high, and would not last the night; it would barely last another hour. It threw great black monsters onto the wall, dancing shadows cast by the imposing four-poster bed set along the long edge of the massive room.

The bed's curtains were closed.

Thoroughly unnerved, Marianne retreated back into the chamber and sat down on a wide, arm-less chair by a round table that wobbled on its thick central leg. Bolton was sitting in a more comfortable gentleman's chair, and packing a pipe with tobacco.

"Rats," he said.

"I beg your pardon?"

He grinned but didn't look up. "This place has rats. I can smell them."

Marianne shivered. The unheated room was sparsely furnished and felt clammy and damp. Mrs Newman had left lamps scattered about for them, but they smoked and smelled. There didn't even seem to be gas laid on to the house.

"I think rats are the least of their problems," she muttered, and drew her shawl tightly around her shoulders. Silently, they waited for the night to close around them.

Two

Bolton wasn't some ardent supporter of New Women and their rights, Marianne decided very quickly. He was just incredibly lazy. He had settled himself quite comfortably in the chair, and Marianne got her notebook and a selection of pens out of her bag. She expected Bolton to start talking to her about the plan for the evening, but he seemed content to simply smoke his pipe. After a little while, Mrs Peck brought in some food on a tray, and put it on a side table. She returned with a large silver teapot and some gold-edged china, and left them to serve themselves.

"Oh, you have first pick," he said, waving his pipe amiably. "Throw whatever you don't want onto a plate for me, miss."

He was the same with the tea. He didn't tell her what to do. But instead he waited, expecting to be served anyway. Marianne rattled the cup against the saucer as she plonked it onto the table in front of him. He smiled and thanked her. He seemed disinclined to do any sort of investigation, or indeed physical movement, but Marianne could not settle. She roamed the room, poking and prodding at the hangings, peeping behind portraits, and looking out of the window to the blank and black night.

The candle in the other room went out.

"My daughter has been writing to a woman physician," Bolton commented, quite out of the blue, as Marianne stood at the connecting door, peering into the gloom. "She has the idea she might train in medicine." He laughed, but mercifully quietly. "I hope she notices men and thinks of marriage before that. I have nothing against it, of course. Makes sense to me, it does. You want a woman doctor dealing with … women's things. Obvious, that."

Marianne could not help herself. She turned and said, "Then why do you want her to notice men, and get married? She won't be able to continue as a doctor if she does."

"Exactly. A wedding's expensive but an education's worse. And if she goes and gets herself trained, that's one lot of money, followed by a wedding which is another lot of money, and all the training for nothing, as she will give up doctoring for being a proper wife and mother. Do you see? Practical man, me."

Marianne sighed. She began to muster her usual rebuttals, ordering her thoughts before she spoke. She had fought hard to finish her studies at Newnham and London, and hated the thought of others having to fight just as hard. She opened her mouth to begin a tirade that she already knew would be futile.

And then they both heard it.

At first, Marianne thought that it was the high-pitched voice of a child, somewhere in a far room, singing in an off-key falsetto. She strode to the closed door that led to the corridor and opened it, thrusting her head out. At the far end of the passage towards the central hall and stairs, a lamp flickered on a table. The noise was no louder out there than it was in the room, so she went back in and prowled around, her head on one side, trying to triangulate the position.

"You hear it too, don't you?" she hissed to Constable Bolton, who had remained seated.

"Oh yes. But that's no ghost," he said, confidently.

"You are right, of course. What is it, do you think?"

"Phonograph, most likely. Or one of those 'graphophone' things. I saw one, once, at an exhibition my missus made us go to."

"Did it sound like this?"

"No. Fancier. Chopin or some such. This is just noise. Does give you the willies, though, don't it?"

Almost as terrifying as female education, she thought. Marianne picked up a small lamp and went carefully to the dark bedroom. She inched her way in through the connecting door. The high voice was not singing; it was more like a recital. There was a rasping edge to it, like whoever was producing the sound could not breathe properly. She held the lamp out and tried to take in the furniture of the room. A device like a phonograph would be easy to spot; they were not small items, with their large flared trumpets atop wooden boxes that housed the wax cylinders.

The curtained bed dominated the room. There were other tables and chairs scattered around but they looked spindly and weak next to the squat, heavy bed. There were black, shadowy pictures on the walls, their moulded frames picking up the light from her lamp. A carved washstand with all the necessaries stood

17

opposite the bed. There was a long, metal-banded chest against the wall, and a chest of drawers next to that.

The noise was coming from the far end of the room, towards the door to the corridor. It was getting increasingly breathless and scratchy. Marianne glanced back at Bolton in the room behind her, but he was watching her with amusement. "You're in charge," he mouthed.

Marianne stepped into the room.

And the noise petered out.

She stopped dead, and listened hard.

A querulous voice came out from behind the curtains. "I know that you're there."

It was an excruciatingly awkward situation for which Marianne was not prepared. She coughed, and said, "Good evening, madam, I…"

The woman in the bed screamed. "Heavens! Oh Lord protect me! Who is there?"

Marianne floundered in confusion. She could hardly march up and fling the drapery aside. She said, "I beg your pardon. Mrs Newman brought me in to investigate the strange noises at night. I thought that you were addressing me when you first spoke. I most humbly beg your forgiveness for disturbing you. I'll go back to the other room. Can I fetch you anything? Be of any assistance?"

"No. Thank you. Oh my! What a shock."

Marianne retreated to the antechamber but paused at the door. "Madam, you said that you knew I was here. To whom were you actually referring?"

"The voice."

"So you hear it too? And what do you think is causing it?"

The answer was terse and snappy. "I don't know. Damp? A broken window? The angry ghosts of my ancestors?"

"Could it be a ghost?" Marianne asked, knowing full well that it could not be.

"*She* thinks so."

"Mrs Newman?"

"Mm. Her. So I think." The voice was faint now and she faded away, hopefully into sleep.

Marianne went back to the table and sat down opposite Constable Bolton, who had not moved an inch. He raised his eyebrows at her, and smiled.

"The plot thickens, eh? Now what, chief?"

"What do you think?" she asked him, experimentally.

He shrugged. "You're in charge. Like I told young Gladstone, I'm happy enough to follow orders. Always the safest way."

You mean that it is the easiest way, you lazy lump, she thought. She wondered if she could order him to show initiative, or whether that would trigger some kind of internal breakdown. Instead she left him alone, and went out into the darkened corridor.

Mrs Newman was coming down the corridor from the main part of the house, with a dark housecoat wrapped around her, and thick woollen slippers on her feet. She still walked with elegance and poise. She had a candle in a holder. "I heard it again," she said in a low voice.

"I heard it too," Marianne said. "I am afraid I might have

woken Miss Dorothea Newman."

"Oh, Miss Dorothea will have woken at the first scream," Mrs Newman said.

"It was not quite screaming, to my ears," Marianne said. "There was a lyrical quality to it. I could not pinpoint the source. Where do you suspect it emanates from?"

"Like you, I am not sure. But it is certainly only heard from the vicinity of the Grand Bedroom."

"And only this part of the house is used?"

"Yes. And mostly only this floor, too. Underneath us in this wing, the rooms are all shut up. The kitchens are at the back of the great hall, and the attics above us are no longer used either."

"Might I be allowed to look around?" Marianne asked, hating the tentative note she could hear in her voice. She ought to be confident. She was here with at the request of the police, after all.

"Of course," Mrs Newman said. "I expected that you would ask. I can accompany you or you can have free rein yourself. I shall inform Mrs Peck in the morning that you are to be allowed full access. She has retired now, I am afraid."

"Oh – I rather thought I might look around now."

"Now? At night?"

"Yes. While the noise is fresh in my ears. It might return."

"No, it never sounds more than once a night." Mrs Newman hesitated and finally said, "Well, if you are sure, then you may. Those two doors at the end, the first you come to by the stairs, are mine and Tobias's rooms."

"Tobias?"

"Ah." Mrs Newman didn't change expression. Her fixed gaze was too telling, in a way. She was repressing something. "Tobias is my poor late husband's nephew. He is but a boy of sixteen, and orphaned. I expect Constable Bolton shall accompany you?"

"I will go and speak to him," Marianne said, and smiled.

Mrs Newman stalked back to her room. Marianne thought, if you call the elder Miss Newman your aunt though she is no blood relation, why do you put a distance between you and this boy, Tobias?

If a recalcitrant kitchen maid isn't causing this mischief, then a young man very well might be.

***

Marianne didn't go back to speak to Constable Bolton. He was of little use. She took a moment to compose herself, and to just listen to the house settling around her. She was not scared.

She told herself that she was not scared a few times, until she started to almost believe it.

Anyway, what was there to be scared of? She did not have any time for spirits, ghosts, phantasms, and anything purporting to come from beyond the veil. She had yet to see a medium who had not relied entirely on tricks and illusions. She hated, with a fierce passion, the abusive tricks played on vulnerable people by those who said they could contact dead loved ones. She was regularly hired by people seeking to expose such tricks, often in the matter of wills and inheritances. After all, fraud was big business. But this was her first official job with the police, and she *had* to get it right.

Maybe that was her fear. That she might fail, and lose the rosy future that she had already been building up in her head. A future she had imagined that was of respect, money and crucially, freedom.

Freedom. Her own house. Hers. That was what she was fighting for: her independence.

She prowled up the corridor, trying every door as she went. None of them were locked. She peeped into a library, a study, a store room, and a well-used day room of comfortable sofas and couches. This was the only recognisably lived-in room she'd seen. It was crowded with familiar objects and decorated in the overblown style of a few decades previously. Even the fireplace was hung with swags of fabric, and every surface was cluttered with clocks and pictures and china ornaments and potted plants. It smelled a little moist.

Nothing suspicious revealed itself in any of the rooms.

She went back to the central hall and found the attic stairs, and crept up to the top floor. A narrow corridor ran the length of the west wing, ending in darkness at the far end, and it was just as Mrs Newman had said. Each room was shut up and unused. Marianne pinpointed the rooms above the Grand Bedroom but they were empty, devoid of everything, with not even a box or a drawer or a plain chair. They were swept clean, and smelled of wood. She went back out to the corridor. The floorboards creaked. She glanced at the far end but the shadows were forbidding and she could not see any doors that she might open. Instead of going to the far end, she retreated.

Marianne explored the rooms underneath the Grand Bedroom then, finding a closed-up withdrawing room and a silent, tomb-like dining room with a massive long table and chairs all covered in sheets.

She lifted every sheet, opened every cabinet and probed into every drawer. Dust surrounded her in clouds and her clothes grew thick with the stuff. She had hoped to find a phonograph laid out on a table, just as Bolton had predicted, but there was nothing, and nowhere that she could see to hide one. She'd look again in the morning, in daylight, if daylight could penetrate the murky windows of Rosedene, but for now, she had to concede defeat.

She slipped quietly upstairs to the room where Bolton was now making himself comfortable in a nest of blankets on the floor.

"You're sleeping?" she asked.

"Why not? If it happens again, I am sure I'll wake up. If I do not, you may hit me with the teapot."

And what use will you be when you wake, she thought. She sat down at the table and waited for the supernatural to come and find her. And she knew that it would not.

Three

Breakfast was awkward, not least because Marianne was exhausted and grubby and knew that she smelled slightly stale. She'd slept, in the end, fitfully, on a long low couch. In hindsight, she was slightly annoyed, mostly with herself. She had been so keen to prove her worth, to show that she was as capable as any policeman, that she had not questioned the actual practicalities of spending the night in the house. Bolton was used to night-time escapades, but she was not. Still, she refused to mention her discomfort. She had an image to maintain. And it was not much worse than her freezing rooms at university, to which she had been confined for long hours and days due to lack of funds or chaperones.

The four of them sat around a small square table in one of the upstairs rooms; Tobias was there. Mrs Newman apologised profusely for the shabby standard of things, explaining that she had not been at Rosedene for long, and had so far made little progress in "improving" the house.

"Not that it's my place to do any such thing," she added. "But for Tobias's sake, you know…" She trailed off.

Tobias was a silent young man with knuckles so knobbly and fingers so thin he looked like he had been made out of pipework and string. He ducked his head when Bolton and Marianne were introduced to him, and didn't say a word. He worked on his eggs with a neat precision, carving them into regulated sections of equal size before eating them with stabs of his fork.

"Tobias," Marianne said, after a few minutes of polite small talk. "Have you heard the strange noises at night?"

He nodded.

"What do you think they are?"

He shrugged.

"Tobias!" Mrs Newman hissed. Then, to Marianne, she said, "Please do allow the boy some slack. He has suffered some personal tragedies of late and ... well. He is not strong. I fear for his heart."

"I am so sorry to hear that," Marianne said, and knew she would not be able to press her question again to the mourning boy without seeming like a monster.

"So," Mrs Newman went on. "Of course, there cannot be a ghost here. Or can there?"

"Of course not. There are no such things. Eminent men and women have been searching for years, but no evidence can be found. Nothing that can be reproduced in a laboratory, anyway," Marianne said.

Mrs Newman nodded. "Quite, quite. So I have read. And yet ... what, then, is causing the disturbance? Dear Aunt Dorothea called in a woman with a talking board, you know, to contact the spirits and ask them to stop. It didn't work, and we were all disappointed."

"No, it wouldn't work. Especially as there are no such things as spirits," Marianne said, looking intently at Mrs Newman. Her impression from the previous night was that Miss Dorothea did not think it was of supernatural origin. Why would she call in a "woman with a talking board" then? "The unconscious wills of the participants influence the board's movements and it spells out only what you want it to spell."

Tobias stirred. He looked about to speak, but instead took a gulp of tea.

"I did not think that the elder Mrs Newman believed in spirits?" Marianne said. "My impression of her was brief, but she was dismissive."

"No, she does not. But much like me, she was and is baffled by the screams. Sometimes it sounds like a voice, a child's voice. When one has explored all everyday explanations, what is one left with?" Mrs Newman laughed with something like embarrassment. "Every day I read of new scientific breakthroughs. Electromagnetism! I saw a demonstration and were it not for the man with a beard and a good suit, I should have thought it to be witchcraft. So here we are. If no cause can be found, then … the truth, however strange, unlikely and awful though it is, must lead us to believe…" She tailed off.

So did Mrs Newman believe, secretly? Many people did. They pretended to be all full of reason but there still seemed to persist, deep in a human heart, the need to believe in something … something *more*. The pain of losing someone was sometimes too much for people to bear. Maybe, they hoped, they were still with us – in spirit.

Marianne understood. But she hated it, nonetheless. Her own mother had never made any kind of visit from "beyond the veil", after all.

Bolton had already finished eating. He patted his lips and sat back, apparently oblivious to the conversation. Mrs Peck materialised to remove the dirty plates, and Tobias took the chance to leap up, mutter something incomprehensible, and quit the room. But he went slowly and awkwardly, noticeably dragging one leg.

"You mentioned a terrible tragedy," Marianne said once he had gone. "Might I ask what happened?"

"He was in a railway accident. Did you not see his limp? His legs were smashed to bits, quite smashed. His parents – my poor dear husband's cousin and his wife – were both killed outright."

Marianne tried to draw out the relationship in her head. So Tobias was not even a nephew, as such, but a more distant relation. "And is he not at school?"

"Not now. He wishes to return, but … well, as you can see, it is all quite impossible. He cannot go back at the moment. Maybe in the future. There are … difficulties. Would you care for more tea?"

"No, thank you. I should like to examine the rooms once more. Including the Grand Bedroom, if Miss Dorothea will allow it."

"Of course, of course."

But nothing more was found, and nothing was hidden, and nothing was revealed. Marianne went through every place with patience and dedicated, and found absolutely nothing that she had not seen during her night time exploration. She caught glimpses of Tobias, in and out of his room and the library, but he did not speak. Dorothea Newman was half-asleep and muttering, and Mrs Peck was busy in the kitchens with a limp maid, and Bolton followed Marianne like a half-beaten dog.

Her head ached. Her body was sore. And she smelled. She gave up before lunch, and trudged back to the railway station with the annoyingly ebullient Bolton. It had begun to rain, only lightly, but every droplet sank into her skirts and made them heavier and heavier. He escorted her to a second class carriage and watched her train pull away, waiting on the platform until she was out of sight.

Marianne sank back into the corner seat, wedged against the window and surrounded by well-dressed women in a group, all on their way to someone's house for some reason that seemed to involve lots of whispered gossip and some unexpected screams of uncouth laughter. She closed her eyes and tried to close her ears to it, and looked forward to a wash, a change of clothes, and an afternoon nap in her own bed at Woodfurlong.

***

She was surprised to find Mr Dry in the hallway when she entered. She was shaking the water off her cape and hat and he hurried forward to help her. He was Price Claverdon's valet and

29

general man, though he would also accompany Phoebe on shopping trips into London if necessary. Marianne was not entirely sure quite how he filled his days. Price worked long days in the city, and especially more so recently. Still, Mr Dry always moved around the house with a busy air, giving off the impression he was buried under a list of duties.

Marianne herself, as half-cousin of Phoebe and living at Woodfurlong at Price and Phoebe's indulgence, had no staff to her name. She let Mr Dry take her wet things with thanks, and asked where the steward or the housekeeper were.

Mr Dry flared his nostrils. "Both are rather *put upon*. Mrs Claverdon's *mother*, Mrs Davenport, is here," he said stiffly and formally. And then, in a lower and more normal voice, "And miss, I must warn you: she is frighteningly intent upon *changes*."

"Oh good heavens, no," Marianne said in alarm.

He glanced around before leaning in even closer to Marianne. "You have a special relationship with the staff, miss. You might reassure them, if you will. She is here *on a mission*."

"What mission?"

He looked at her closely and there was a flicker of unease in his eyes. "Against *extravagance*," he whispered, and paled, and looked around again, as if he were about to be set upon.

And perhaps he was, in a sense.

Marianne understood, and felt a cold fear grip her own heart, too. She nodded, and started out for the Garden Wing, where she lived with her chronically ill father and his chemical experiments.

She nearly made it before being ambushed.

The central hallway of Woodfurlong was designed to impress and to welcome guests and strangers alike. It had a large central staircase that swept upwards, interrupted by a landing area halfway where it then split into two curling sets of stairs heading to a gallery lined with cabinets that showed Phoebe and Price's wealth and good taste. This meant it was difficult to make an unseen entrance, especially if the door to the drawing room upstairs was left open. In this case, it clearly had been, and deliberately so.

Mrs Ann Davenport, Phoebe's mother, swooped down the stairs and hailed Marianne. Marianne could not pretend to ignore her.

"We've been waiting for you, Marianne!" Mrs Davenport declared. She gripped the handrail tightly but walked upright and stiffly, determined not to let her age slow her down at all. Phoebe fluttered behind, pulling faces at Marianne that she could not decipher. But they weren't ones of joy, at any rate.

Mrs Davenport reached the ground floor and extended her fingers for Marianne to press. They were as dry and papery as the woman herself. She was dressed in shades of grey and cream, in the fashion of three years ago. Her clothing was always of such quality that it never wore out and needed replacing. She wore tiny, exquisite jewels that were priceless heirlooms. She would never have shopped for such things herself.

And she despised someone who would.

Vanity and avarice were such worldly sins.

"Marianne," she said, in a voice that was carefully kind and warm. The calculation of it, the theatrical artifice, made Marianne wince. "My dear girl. How you've … grown."

Marianne felt as if she was too tall, and that she had deliberately done it to annoy Mrs Davenport. Phoebe and Marianne were half-cousins, and after the death of Marianne's mother, they had spent much of their childhood together. Yet Mrs Davenport was never going to be anything other than the strictly formal Mrs Davenport. It was even an effort for Phoebe to call her *mother*.

"Mrs Davenport. How lovely to see you. And unexpected. I hope you are keeping well?"

"Tolerably so. I thank the Lord every day for my good fortune, my family, my household and my gifts."

"As do I."

"Hmm."

They both knew that Marianne was lying.

Mrs Davenport swept her critical eye across Marianne and clearly disapproved of her crumpled, stale-smelling state. Although to be fair, Marianne disapproved of her own state too. "And I understand that tragically you are still unwed," Mrs Davenport said, as if referring to a bad case of haemorrhoids.

"I have been busy with my studies and now, my work occupies much of my time."

"When you marry, you will have far more important work to do." She smiled thinly. "As you are well aware, I am sure. You know your duty. To the country. I do think it is only fear that is holding you back. But you must fear no longer. I am here to help."

"Oh – please do *not* trouble yourself on my account," Marianne said. Her fear increased tenfold.

32

Phoebe finally came to Marianne's defence. She came to her mother's side and took her arm. "Marianne is fully aware of her duties and don't forget, she is responsible for her father and she takes that very seriously. What better duty than that of a daughter?"

Well, thought Marianne, I do prevent him from burning the place down on a weekly basis.

Mrs Davenport wrinkled her nose. She would prefer to forget about Russell Starr, errant chemist, altogether. She said, "Well, I shan't detain you further, or you will have no time to change for lunch. I look forward to continuing our discussion then."

Not likely. Marianne routinely changed her clothes for dinner, but she had no intention of even attending lunch with the others, never mind changing an extra time. "I am afraid I have other ... duties ... which will keep me in my rooms for the rest of the day. Good day, madam."

She escaped at last, but she had only just got to her own room when Phoebe caught up with her. Phoebe bundled her quickly into the room and slammed the door shut behind her.

Marianne sighed. "Phoebe, oh please, just let me wash and eat and sleep. You have no idea of the night I've had. Honestly. I've not slept a wink."

"Oh, the screaming! Yes, yes. It will be some child playing a prank and you know it. You will have found them out already, I am sure. Listen to what I am dealing with. It is true horror, I am telling you. True horror! Marianne, we must act before it is too late!"

Marianne rolled her eyes. "Phoebe, go away. I swear that I am about to collapse in a heap."

"Come here. Turn around." Phoebe began to help Marianne out of her clothes, which were still damp from the rain and massed in thick and unwieldly layers. Phoebe tugged and unhooked and unlaced as she talked. "I know this is all my fault, but I am sorry. No, actually, I shall blame Price. It is his fault. Not the rain. I mean, my mother. Do you want me to call for a bath for you?"

"No, thank you."

"Good, for mother would have a fit if she knew. I am quite cross with Price, quite cross. I barely spoke to him this morning. But I don't think he noticed as he was reading his newspaper. But still, I made my point, I am sure."

"Why is she here, Phoebe?"

"Oh, it's such an ugly tale. I can't bear to tell you."

"Be strong. Speak out."

"All right, then."

Marianne went behind a screen and found a clean shift and a comfortable housecoat to wear. She intended to nap for a few hours. Phoebe prattled on after seating herself on a couch by the window. "Ever since that business with the Prussians, Price has been worried about money. It's such nonsense. He's always had money, and I don't understand why he is thinking it might all go away. It's not like water, rushing down a drain."

Marianne laughed. "You innocent buffoon. It is exactly like water! You just don't understand because you've always had it. Money's like the ocean to you. It's endless."

"Well, anyway, I don't need to understand it. Except that he has been talking to other people, and other men's wives, and apparently I am considered to be *frivolous*. As if that is a bad thing."

"Yes, but you are. And yes, it is."

"It's not fair! He says I am to make better household decisions. I asked him to be specific. He said that he could not, as it was not his realm, and he did not care to be bothered by matters of the female sphere."

"That is just his way of saying he doesn't have a clue, either."

"Oh, I know that," Phoebe said. "So I am to budget, but I do not know how. He suggested I ask my mother to stay, and I thought that it would be all right. She has been positively dying to come and be all matronly over me for a long time. As soon as she arrived this morning, I knew that I had made a mistake in asking her. And I doubt that she will go home again until she has thoroughly overhauled the whole place. We are now a project for her. She must succeed and overcome. Victory will be hers."

"Dry told me that the staff are worried."

"Of course they are. She is like the grim reaper, come to harvest money instead of souls. She brings the economy of doom. She says there are too many staff here. Well, how should I manage with fewer? I have no idea. Everyone has their role. It is impossible. Marianne, I hate to bother you with more chores, but can you poison her?"

"Absolutely not. Phoebe, please, I need to sleep. I am about to fall down."

Finally, Phoebe registered Marianne's truly exhausted state. "Oh dear. I'll have some cold food sent in. You get into bed, right now! And don't worry about what my mother said. Although she has a point. If you got married, you'd stop her trying to match-make for you…"

Where had that threat come from? Marianne was alarmed. "I'll poison the pair of you if either of you meddle in my love life. Do not let her."

"You don't have a love life to meddle in." Phoebe got up and went to the door. "I'll speak to cook. Meat, bread, fruit?" she asked as she opened it. "A little wine?"

Mrs Davenport stepped in, surprising them both.

Phoebe stifled a yelp and put her hand to her throat. Marianne stood behind her bed, clutching her housecoat around herself. "Um…?"

Mrs Davenport did not look at Marianne. She said to her daughter, "Meat, bread, fruit? And wine? Phoebe, this is one more example of your lack of awareness. I have already been to the kitchens, and I found the most shocking display of wanton disregard for propriety. The cook was feeding an errand boy! He had come to deliver some fish, and she was treating him like a member of the family. With *your* food that *your husband* has paid for. This must stop. I will deal with this issue myself. You will have a queue of unfortunates at your door at all hours if this does not stop. As for the lack of respect your cook shows…"

"Mother…"

"Come along. I shall show you how this must be handled." Mrs Davenport whirled around and hauled Phoebe out with her.

Marianne sank onto her bed, and pulled a blanket over herself. She was too tired to fret about it all at the moment, and she let herself swim into sleep.

Four

Marianne was awoken by the sounds of banging and shouting. She lay in her bed, listening, wondering if the staff had staged a rebellion and were even now chasing Mrs Davenport from the house. If so, she ought to jump up and join them in their endeavour. She had always fancied wielding a pitchfork as part of a mob.

As her head cleared, she focused more clearly on the sound of her father's voice, and the answering shouts of Mrs Olive Crouch, his nurse.

Mrs Crouch could handle herself. She'd terrified whole regiments of men in the Crimea, if her tales were to be believed. Marianne rolled out of bed and did not hurry in washing and dressing. It was mid-afternoon, and her mouth was dry, and her eyes scratched and itched. No food had been delivered; Phoebe's mother must have vetoed it. She wondered how long the intolerable woman was going to stay.

Poison could perhaps be an option. Not to kill, but perhaps to make her a little ill? Ill enough to want to go home?

Marianne felt guilty but it didn't stop the thought.

Her room was one of a small suite that had been given over to her and her father. She wandered out into the corridor and followed the noise, tracking it to her father's day room. She listened at the door.

He was in a rage about the sun. That made as much sense as it ever did. Last week, he had hallucinated beetles all over his skin and he had had to be put into a deep sleep before he scratched his own flesh off.

Mrs Crouch was having none of his raving about the light. "Take your medication and be done with it. I shall draw the curtains then, sir, and not before. Now, drink this!"

Russell spoke thickly, and she knew that the mercury doses he was taking were making him drool and spit up more saliva than should have been humanly possible. He ranted back at her about his eyes, his mouth, his skin, his youth, his studies, his enemies in the Royal Society, the French, and the current government. Marianne started to open the door, caught sight of Mrs Crouch levering the pills into his mouth as he foamed and spat, and thought better of it. She retreated before she could be seen.

Weariness washed over her. She leaned against the wall and sighed.

No. She would *not* mope. Moping had never achieved a thing. She pushed herself upright and forced herself to go out for a walk. The rain had stopped, and she needed clear air for a clear head.

The arrival of Ann Davenport was a signal to Marianne that she needed to leave this house, more than ever. Her father's illness complicated matters, but that was a burden she had to bear. As for the failure at Rosedene, she was smarting about that. But really, with the useless lump of a constable by her side, she had been set up to fail! Yes, she had heard the strange noises and yes, they did indeed sound like screams. But that was all she could declare about it.

She knew the police had searched the house thoroughly. She herself had done so, too; twice.

But it was not enough. She could not leave it at that. Not only for her own professional pride, and the irksome nature of an unanswered question but – and here, she chastised herself again for being so crass – but she needed the money.

Only money could release her from living under her cousin's roof.

She had made plans. She had charts showing projected income and rent and possible expenditure and cheap but respectable places she might choose to live. She had *goals* – not dreams.

She darted back inside to fetch her outdoor walking clothes, and change into sturdy boots. She had to meet with Inspector Gladstone soon, and she had some things to say to the man.

***

Unlike Rosedene, Woodfurlong was handily placed for the railway and she was able to reach the middle of London easily within half an hour. Inspector Gladstone listened, most seriously, to her reflections and demands.

He agreed to everything she asked, and sent a message to Mrs Newman at Rosedene. The day was slipping away, and Marianne did not have time to wait for a reply. She went back to Woodfurlong, dozing on the train, pleaded a headache, and took to her rooms, knowing that Mrs Davenport would spend the evening telling Price and Phoebe that she'd brought it on herself. Reading books, and thinking, was doing Marianne no good at all. Her brain was overheating in a most unfeminine way, no doubt.

She slept well, regardless.

A message was brought to Marianne the following day. She read it, punched the air because nobody was looking, and stifled her unseemly shout of glee, because people would always be listening. She avoided Mrs Davenport, who spent the whole day closeted with Phoebe and the household accounts. Even the staff slipped around with silent, long faces, each one worried for their positions.

It was true that they kept an extravagantly large household at Woodfurlong. No one else that they knew had quite so many staff. Price was rich – he had inherited wealth and he made it, too. But was he rich enough? Did they really need Mr Dry, who was Price's valet *and* Mr Barrington, the house steward? Two male "indoor" servants, really? Plus the cook and the seething coterie of maids, the housekeeper and the children's nurse, Russell's nurse, Phoebe's lady's maid and the various outdoor staff – gardeners, coachman, stable boy? The Claverdons were well-to-do but they were certainly not the very upper classes. They had no title and no ancient pockets of land dotted around.

Although it had to be said that Mrs Davenport's objections were not strictly to do with money, but rather with how such extravagance looked to others. People, she said, would judge them, and such ostentatious displays of wealth were simply unseemly.

It would not *do*.

Marianne sneaked into the kitchens just after lunch and found Mrs Cogwell the cook close to tears. "I should love to find you some food, my dear," she said in a low voice. "But it is all put away – put away! Locked up, as if I am a common thief. I have never stolen a thing in my life, and you know it."

"I don't need sugar or tea," Marianne told her. "Just a little bread, perhaps? Some cheese?"

Mrs Cogwell shook her head and her jowls wobbled. "Everything is to be accounted for, now. The menus are planned out, just as I have always done, but now mistress is to count out what is to be used, and no more! Not one ounce more! She vows she will even examine what is thrown away. Miss, might you have a word with her?"

"I do not think my word would be heard. But don't worry. She cannot stay here for ever."

"She said that she will stay until her work here is done. And begging pardon, miss, but you are to be part of that work, so I hear."

"I see," Marianne said grimly. "Do not fret about me. I will get some food in town."

"I didn't mean food, miss. I mean she has in mind to …"

Marianne knew what she meant. This marriage nonsense

again. She stamped out into the gathering chill of the autumn afternoon.

Five

She loved London, at any time of the day or night. It hummed with life. She was poor enough to be able to pass unnoticed through many of the streets, during the daytime at least. Phoebe could never walk alone here, though the pair of them together could visit the better sorts of shops and even the new tea rooms springing up to cater for women with money and time, and nothing better to do with either of those things.

At the turn of the day, as the light faded, the atmosphere changed. Marianne took more care about where she went, and when. She was not painted enough to pass as a jade, nor shabby enough to be completely ignored as the sun went down and the nightlife came out. But by the time that danger was emerging, she was already once more at Rosedene, and this time she was alone. Constable Bolton had been of no use. She was going to do this alone.

Mrs Newman herself answered the door and let her into the cold, dark hall. "Miss Starr, how delightful to see you again. I only wish it were under more favourable circumstances."

"I do understand. I was troubled by what I heard last time,

and I am very grateful that you have allowed me back to conduct a more thorough search." She was convinced that she had missed something, somehow.

"And this time, you have brought supplies! Scientific instruments, no doubt?"

"Indeed." Marianne's arm was aching from carrying the heavy bag. She had a blanket with her, but more importantly, she had various tools and powders too. She was determined to track down the source of the noise as soon as it began. "I wonder if I might beg your indulgence in one more matter. It is somewhat sensitive."

"Please, do not hesitate. I, like you, am keen to get to the bottom of things."

"It is about the boy, Tobias."

"Yes?"

"The only occupants here are yourself, the housekeeper Mrs Peck, Miss Dorothea Newman, and the boy, is that correct? No maids?"

"A girl comes in daily, but you are right. There are just us four, rattling around. Well, my dear aunt does not rattle, but you know what I mean."

"Indeed. How long has Tobias been here?"

"Just over a year."

"That long! What of his future? You mentioned that you thought he might return to school but if he has not done so in a year, then…"

"I fear his future is sad and utterly without prospect, in truth. I do not know what my aunt might plan for him. He cannot return to school simply because there is no money for that, and my heart breaks for him. It is an indelicate subject. Pardon me, but I do not like to speak of it."

"And so what of his own plans?"

"I do not know. What could he do, anyway? When you were here before, he was not sullen and silent because of your presence. He is always like that. He is a most unpersonable boy."

"But he has lost his parents and suffered the trauma of an unspeakable accident."

"It was many months ago. He is prone to lingering in grief. Men must pull themselves together and carry on. I wish he had more of the firm Newman character, and then a position might yet be found for him, but it is not to be. Do you think...?"

Marianne nodded. "Yes, my suspicions lie with him. Has he spent any time away, while you have been here?"

"No. If I could have sent him away, I would have done so. For his own good, of course. Alas..."

"I am going to ask if he might be locked into his room tonight," Marianne said. "I hate to suggest it, but it is one way to perhaps rule him out."

Mrs Newman looked doubtful, but she nodded. "I see. Yes. I shall not tell him. I shall simply do it. I have never caught him prowling at night, so I daresay he won't even notice."

Marianne was uncomfortable with it, but she thanked Mrs Newman, and they went up to the rooms on the first floor. Mrs Newman brought her some refreshments, and left her alone.

Once again, Marianne felt the strange awkwardness of being in the next room to a confined invalid to whom she had not been properly introduced. She could hear a light snoring. She moved as quietly as she could, laying out the implements that she had brought with her.

There had to be human agency behind the noise. That much was a given. So, who was doing it? First she had to rule out every person who officially lived in the house. Mrs Newman herself had raised the issue with the police, but did that make her innocent? Marianne was not prepared to dismiss her so lightly but she did not want to make Mrs Newman aware of her suspicions. Marianne would have to watch her, and Mrs Peck, also, who slept in a tiny room by the kitchen. If Tobias was safely locked into his room, that would help.

And then there was Dorothea Newman, the old lady herself, the owner of the house. Everyone else was here with her permission, really. Mrs Newman must have had her agreement to involve the police.

When Marianne had heard the noise, it had very clearly not been coming from the curtained bed. But she had in mind a system of tubes, and pipes, and rubber, and all manner of ways to make a sound be transmitted from one area to another. Quite *why* anyone should do such a thing was another matter. And that was why Marianne suspected Tobias most of all. To a lonely boy, suffering trauma, trapped in a house where he wasn't really welcome, with an uncertain future, anything might count as entertainment.

Mrs Newman had told Marianne that Tobias would take to his room after dinner, around eight that evening, and not reappear until breakfast the next morning. Marianne waited in the room, and heard the footsteps of the boy going to bed. They were followed a little later by another set of much stealthier treads, and the little click of a key in a lock. He must have heard it. Marianne waited for a furious banging or shouting or some kind of protest, but nothing happened. She went to the corridor and peeked out, and saw Mrs Newman's own door close at the far end. Both rooms were far away from where she had heard the noises. The house was not laid for water or gas, and did not have the snakes of pipes that many houses were now sprouting. It would be difficult to create a sound in those bedrooms and have it appear down at this end of the corridor.

Difficult, but not impossible.

She went back and picked a few things from the table. Tobias was locked in, but she wanted to safeguard Mrs Newman too. She took a few fine hairs that she had plucked from her own hairbrush earlier, and went out into the corridor with a small pot of rabbit skin glue and a horsehair paintbrush, stiff and solid.

She painted the glue onto the doorframes and the doors, and sealed Tobias and Mrs Newman into their rooms. She then worked her way back along the corridor, repeating the procedure with every door.

That done, she picked up a small box filled with cornflour. She had bought this when passing through town, now that all the food at Woodfurlong was being kept under lock and key. She'd heard of the practice of stringent economy and it was commonly recommended in household manuals, but it seemed like an awfully inefficient way to run a kitchen, and terribly insulting to the cook who had been in the family for decades.

Also, it severely hampered her erratic approach to mealtimes now that she couldn't just wander into the kitchens and find food at any time of the day or night.

She laid the cornflour in long thin lines, arcing around the entrance to Dorothea's room in the corridor, and also the other doors nearby. This had been the area where the screams had sounded the loudest. If a door opened, and the hairs broke, the cornflour should show her the direction that the perpetrator passed. In the gloom of the corridor, the lines were insubstantial and almost invisible. Only she knew that they were there.

Then she moved her chair to the doorway so that she could settle and watch the corridor, particularly to the left in the direction of the door to Dorothea's chamber.

She waited.

There were two lamps in the room behind her but their light didn't extend very well to the corridor. Her eyes were adjusted to the darkness and she would be able to see shapes, and that was enough. She feared that if she lit it too much, she would scare away the person responsible.

She wondered, then, why the source of the noise had continued in their silly play when she and Constable Bolton had been there. They must have been confident they would not be found out. Would they put in a repeat performance this night?

She found out an hour later.

It started like a nursery rhyme but quickly grew high and screeching. Marianne shot to her feet, her heart thumping. Nothing moved but the noise was coming from her left. She went towards it. She pressed her ear to the closed door of the

Grand Bedroom, but the screaming did not sound any louder. She was sure now that it was coming from the opposite side of the corridor. She inched towards a door. It was wide, with dark wood panels, a real Tudor relic. Her cornflour had not been disturbed and the hair was unbroken.

The noise was definitely coming from within. She cast her mind back to her previous visit. It was just a storeroom. There had been nothing interesting in there.

It was, therefore, the ideal place to hide.

If the malefactor had secreted themselves *before* she had set her traps, then this made perfect sense. There could be another person involved here, known or unknown to the other occupants. Annoyed, now, rather than scared, she flung the door open just as the noise died away.

It was pitch black inside. She shot back to her room, grabbed a lamp, and returned. No one could have escaped out in the time that it took her to move, or she would surely have heard them, but she cursed herself anyway. She should have got the lamp before she opened the door.

Nothing stirred. She strode into the room and hissed, "Who's there? Come on. This is a silly joke that has gone too far."

She held the lamp high and examined every inch of the room. There were three round tables, and each one was piled with dusty objects – books, dolls, a box of toy soldiers, a hat with torn silk flowers. There was a large upturned glass that might have housed ferns at one point. A broken clock lay on the floor. Two chairs were tumbled onto their backs.

But there was nowhere for anyone to hide.

She went to the armoire, thinking that as it was against an adjoining wall, it might have a false back, allowing someone to sneak from room to room. It was full of old fur coats, and smelled dreadful, but the wooden back was solid and did not come loose to her prying fingers.

Then she passed to the window. It was a simple style with one latch, unlocked, and it opened easily. She craned her head out but there was no balcony that could have afforded easy access from outside.

She was baffled. And she hated it. She kicked at the floorboards, and looked up at the ceiling, and tapped the wooden walls, but they all sounded hollow to her with no differences from wall to wall.

She put the lamp on a table and picked up the broken clock, shaking it, hoping that it might producing some kind of sound. Perhaps its chiming mechanism was still half-functional. Nothing happened. She shook out the toy soldiers all over the floor, but there was nothing hidden at the bottom of the box. She peeked under the doll's skirts but there was only the expected bloomers and stiff china legs. It rattled as its head fell forward, its articulated neck now rusted and stiff. She put it down, unnerved by its unblinking gaze.

Nothing, nothing, nothing. She snatched up the lamp and looked up at the ceiling again. Had that been a noise, a scratch or a slither, up above her in the empty attics?

It was a tiny lead, but it was all she had to go on.

As she went along the corridor, she checked the flour on

the floor and hair over each door. No one had stirred. She crept up the stairs and stopped as she got to the top, before she rounded the sharp corner that led out to the passageway. Once, the household's servants had lived up here, and possibly even the nursery or schoolroom had been here, in this wing or the other one.

There was another noise that came from further down the corridor. It was a click, small and sharp and oddly final. She drew in her breath and wished, unexpectedly, that Constable Bolton was with her. He was useless, but he was at least a presence. She was nervous about being alone. Although, she was also nervous that she might be about to find out that she wasn't on her own at all.

She peeked around the corner, bringing the light of the lamp with her. Something shot along the floor towards her, brushing against her skirts, and skittered away. She would have screamed but her mouth was too dry, and her heart hammered so loudly she couldn't hear anything else.

A rat. It had been nothing but a rat. She forced herself to calm down. Goodness knows, she'd seen plenty of rats in her time. She lived in London, for heaven's sake. She had a few more stern words with herself and then something occurred to her.

What had startled the rat to make it run *towards* her?

She had explored this corridor before, but she did so again, walking slowly and steadily down the centre of the uncarpeted passage, zigzagging from room to room, peeping into every space.

Click.

The noise came from below her foot and she froze in place, staring down at the wooden boards. Then she looked up and this time, she did squeak in surprise.

Two glowing green dots – eyes! They were eyes! – were watching her from the far end of the corridor.

If she were a rat, she'd run too.

But she was not a rat. She held the lamp high in her shaking hand. The dots resolved themselves in a black mass, darker than the shadows around it.

"Oh. Oh! Here, puss, puss," she said. She took one step forward and the click sounded again, and the eyes closed abruptly.

She went on, thrusting the lamp out in front of her. The cat did not move. In fact, as she got close to it, she realised it was never going to move. It had not twitched, or run, or caught a rat in a very long time. She put the lamp on the floor and squatted by the stuffed animal, and reached out to tentatively touch it. It was solid, and cold, and unnervingly lifelike. The lamp's light was reflected in two glass beads set where its eyes had once been.

But they had lit up. They had lit up at the same time as the click had sounded. She nearly laughed. She stood up and pushed at the thing with her foot, not wanting to touch it again with her bare skin. It moved slightly, and revealed a wire that ran from underneath its belly and into a crack between two floorboards.

She left it as it was, and retraced her steps, probing each step until she found the spot that had triggered the cat's eyes again. Click. And the green light shone out. She shook her head and laughed to herself. She had read about a similar experiment in an issue of Popular Mechanic magazine; the owner of a stately home with a rat problem had created exactly this kind of thing. She knelt and found that the floorboard was loose. She prised it up and there it was, just as she expected; the other end of the wire, and a small gap between them. A large and ungainly set of batteries was next to it. The circuit was completed when something pressed down. The space was very tiny, and easily triggered by a fat rat. Her own footstep had pressed it even further, hence the audible click, and the wire was now bent, but the circuit still completed and let the current flow.

She admired it. And she knew exactly who had made this device. It must have been the work of the lonely, silent Tobias. She replaced everything exactly as she found it, and went back downstairs to sit at the table in the side room, and ponder the situation.

She had not found the cause of the screams. It irked her. But it was clearly linked to the boy's clever antics, and as far as she was concerned, this proved everything.

Almost everything.

She poured herself a little rhubarb cordial from the tray of things that Mrs Peck had brought to her, and wrapped the blanket around her shoulders, and tried to work out how *she* would recreate night time screaming if she were a bored young man in an empty house. He had knowledge of electrical matters, and a practical and inventive mind; and he obviously read Popular Mechanic.

There was one more question that she tried to ignore. The rat-scarer had a clear purpose. So what exactly was the screaming supposed to achieve?

The boy had shown himself to be precise and practical. She had to work out why he would do such strange things.

Six

Marianne woke as the morning light filtered through the window. She hadn't drawn the curtains, and the day promised to be one of those bright, clear, sharp days that made her think of mulled cider and ginger biscuits and the approach of the festive season. She was curled on the couch, and stiff in all her limbs. It was a solidly stuffed piece of furniture with wooden arms and a thinly upholstered back, and only really designed for perching upon with one's skirts spread out prettily. She rolled to her feet and stretched and yawned. At least she'd had some sleep this time.

She went out and found a thin young woman carrying a bucket of ashes, and asked her if she might bring warm water to her room. This time, when Marianne went to join Mrs Newman at breakfast, she was feeling a little more human, having had a wash.

Tobias kept his head bowed.

Mrs Newman did the serving, in a gracious way, leaving Mrs Peck and the girl to see to things in the kitchen. Once they were all settled in their places, she asked if Marianne had made any progress.

Marianne glanced at Tobias as she said, "Yes, I have. I've made a startling discovery about what is going on here."

The boy made no movement save for the lifting of his fork to his mouth. But Mrs Newman straightened up. "Oh! Oh?"

"Tobias," Marianne said. "You are a clever boy. Did you enjoy practical matters when you were at school? You were sent away to school, weren't you?"

He nodded but didn't say anything.

"Until the accident, yes, he was away in the country," Mrs Newman said. "Sadly, as we discussed, circumstances have left him rather unable to return. At present."

At present? Mrs Newman had said it was due to the financial situation. That wouldn't improve, and she knew that feeling well. Perhaps Mrs Newman was trying to hide the impossibility of returning to school from him, but that was surely wrong in the long term. Anyway, the boy was not stupid and he would surely be aware of what stood in his way. She said, "But you're continuing to study and keep busy, aren't you, Tobias?"

He nodded again.

"And your latest project has a noble aim. You are ridding Rosedene of rats, isn't that right?"

He looked up at her in surprise. He had light hazel-coloured eyes, and skin so pale she thought he might burn up red on a winter's day if he stepped outside into the sun.

"Rats?" Mrs Newman said sharply.

"Forgive me. An old house like this cannot fail to have its share of pests and creatures. But Tobias has been very clever in setting up a little electrical trick in the attic to scare them away. I am impressed," she added, addressing Mrs Newman. "He has done it perfectly and with great skill."

Mrs Newman put her cutlery down very carefully. She said, in a frighteningly level voice, "Tobias. What have you done?"

He muttered, "Scaring off rats, like she said."

Marianne did not want the lad to be in trouble. She hastily described the whole set-up, praising his cleverness and ingenuity in what he had managed to create, and its efficiency too.

Eventually, Mrs Newman said, "Well, then. I can see the reasoning, at least, but Tobias; you really should have told me what you were doing. And now, what about the noises? They cannot be linked, surely?"

Marianne kept her eyes on Tobias. "I would wager that they are."

He looked up again, and made direct eye contact. "No, they are not! They are nothing to do with me, nothing."

"I am not blaming you," Marianne said. "I only suggest that they might be a by-product of your experiments, that is all."

"No," he said flatly. "There is no circumstance that would make those noises. Nothing of *my* doing."

Marianne turned to Mrs Newman. "Perhaps…"

But Mrs Newman shook her head, too. "No. For all his faults, this boy is not a liar. He is the most honest lad I have met. If he says that he has not caused the noise, then he has not. Which only leaves one conclusion, as we discussed before." She raised her chin and looked at the ceiling, affecting an air of crushed despair.

Marianne was surprised at Mrs Newman's words. The previous night, she'd called Tobias "the most unpersonable boy" she had ever met, alluding to his lack of character. Now she was defending him in the face of all reason.

"The only conclusion is that someone else is making the sound," Marianne said. "Either accidentally or deliberately." Perhaps she ought to look to Mrs Peck. Although how the housekeeper had got from her room to the corridor, and why she was causing such chaos, was such a mystery that it was exceedingly unlikely.

"Well," said Mrs Newman, "Who would that be? My dear aunt cannot leave her bed. Initially, she called for mediums to help but they could not. They used the talking board, as I told you, but got nothing but gibberish. At her behest, I called the authorities, suspecting foul play, and they found nothing. They involved you, a specialist in trickery and illusions, which I supported, and you have discovered nothing. I am a sceptical woman, as you know, and I am not comfortable with my conclusion but…"

"But you are saying that the noise does have a supernatural origin?"

"I do not want to believe it. I cannot believe it. And yet I can no longer see any other option. We must accept it, at last."

Marianne shook her head. "There must be something else. Might I speak to Miss Dorothea Newman before I leave? Would you introduce me?"

***

Mrs Newman went to prepare her aunt for Marianne's visit. Marianne followed and waited in the corridor, listening hard to Mrs Newman's conversation, but it all seemed entirely innocent. Dorothea Newman spoke in a quivering voice. "Do you mean the woman who startled me the other night? She said that she was with the police. A lady-clerk? A police matron? Oh, no? Very well, then."

So she retains her memory, thought Marianne, and seems perfectly lucid. Marianne was shown in, and Mrs Newman fussed over the pillows before leaving quietly.

Marianne assumed she would linger in the corridor and eavesdrop, of course.

Miss Dorothea Newman was nothing more than a wrinkled face surrounded by fabric and frills. She had a cotton lace-edged nightcap covering her head completely, and a high-necked gown that poked out above the layers of sheets and blankets, topped off with a stitched sateen quilt in the Durham style, all curling leaves picked out in tiny stitches. Her eyes were small, pale and bright.

"Well?" she said. "Come closer. I can barely see you."

Marianne moved to the side of the bed, feeling awkward. Phoebe would have been holding the woman's hands by now, and showering her with warm platitudes. Marianne was a harder sort, and she regretted that, but such was her nature. She'd learned her bedside manner from Mrs Crouch, after all. "Can you see me now?" she asked.

"Hmph. You're less of a blob now."

"Miss Newman, I heard that noise again last night. Did

you?"

"Yes. Dreadful screaming. Oh, do call me Dorothea. I am too old for fanciness."

"Thank you. Does it ever happen more than once a night?"

"No. And once it's done, it's done."

"Does it occur at the same time each night?"

"No. And that drive me quite, quite mad. One is so on edge, you see, waiting. Waiting for it. I cannot rest now until it has been and gone. Then I can sleep."

"Does it happen every night?"

"No. Most nights, though. It is a torture! If it does not happen, I do not sleep at all; I am waiting, all night for it."

"And how long has it been happening?" She dropped her voice and leaned in so that the old lady could still hear her, but eavesdroppers outside could not. "Since Mrs Newman arrived, perhaps?"

"No, no," Miss Dorothea said. "She has been here for many months, but the noise started up only very recently."

"And yet, have you any suspicions of her?" Marianne recalled that the previous time, Miss Dorothea hadn't seemed to speak warmly of Mrs Newman – although she had just had a midnight fright.

"No," Miss Dorothea said. "I do not suspect her of anything. She is as frightened as I am."

"And the boy?"

"He has been here over a year. There can be no connection. He is a poor, troubled lad."

"Then actually, he is very likely to be the culprit," Marianne said. "If only he could be sent back to school…" As she said it, she realised that was the perfect explanation for everything. He was a clever boy, after all. Perhaps he was manufacturing a mysterious noise, knowing he'd be suspected, and knowing he would be sent away to test such theories. They had been played, simply played by the boy.

How clever.

But Miss Dorothea was still shaking her head. "No, she has said that is impossible."

"For him to have conjured up the noise, or to be sent to school?"

"He is a good lad. A good lad. I will see him right."

"If the money could be found…"

Miss Dorothea coughed in indignation. "It's all tied up in the house. If I could help him, I would. I promise you that. I would. There might be a way, if I sell some items, but she … oh, you know."

It was a delicate matter and a private one. She let it drop.

Marianne could not think of anything else to ask her. Miss Dorothea's bird-claw hand was poking out from the sheets, and Marianne patted it awkwardly, about to take her leave.

Miss Dorothea's fingers gripped her hand suddenly and Marianne was dragged closer to her face.

"There *is* something else in this house."

"There are rats," Marianne said. "Above you, in the attic. I am sorry to tell you, but don't be alarmed."

"I am not talking about rats. I am old. I know about rats. I know their sound. There is something else."

"A person? Someone hiding?"

"Not someone. Some*thing*."

"What? What have you seen, what have you heard?" Marianne said.

Miss Dorothea let go and Marianne heard a cough behind her in the corridor. Mrs Newman had returned. "Is everything all right? It had gone quiet and I was worried."

"Of course, of course. I think your aunt is tired. I am so sorry if I have over-taxed her."

With a flurry of apologies, Marianne gathered up her things from the antechamber, and let herself be escorted out of the house. She wondered about Miss Dorothea's final words, and studied the younger Mrs Newman, and decided not to ask her any further questions.

She could not go to Inspector Gladstone and request yet more time. Her investigation had failed. She still suspected Tobias to be behind it all, but she was longing to know why. The school theory was tenuous at best and she would have been embarrassed to even try to explain it to anyone else.

She would have to let it go.

Seven

"Letting things go is not my strongest suit," Marianne complained to her friend Simeon.

He laughed. "On the contrary. I'd argue that it's your best trait!"

She pouted and looked around for something to throw at him, and then thought better of it. Nothing was as it seemed in the stage magician's abode. He rented two rooms above a tailor's workshop in London, a veritable palace of space for one person alone, and here he created illusions both large and small. The place was a huge trap for the unwary. If she threw a ball, it would probably unfurl into a peacock while it was still in the air.

"It is," Simeon insisted. "What would have got you through your studies at university if not your dogged determination? What would have got you to London to take your degree at last, if not bloody-mindedness? What would keep you at your father's side even when he is unwell? What would have kept you going when you were starting out as a professional investigator? If you were inclined to let things go, you would not be the success that you are now. You'd be a wife and a mother and unhappy. You'd turn to drink and laudanum and possibly affairs and scandal."

It was almost sounding appealing – the drink and scandal part, at any rate. "Yet I am not a success," she said mulishly. "I am poor and I have failed in my latest task. Now I must return to the police and tell them I cannot solve it. Then I will go home and face Phoebe's mother. She is intent on marrying me off, and turning Phoebe into the perfectly moderate housewife, a shining example of Christian frugality and restraint."

"Good heavens," Simeon said, feigning an attack of the vapours as he clutched his throat with one hand and pressed the back of his other to his forehead, staggering against a tall wooden cabinet. "She must be some kind of miracle-working saint, for those two tasks are surely impossible."

"What can I throw at you that won't come apart in the air?" Marianne said crossly.

"Nothing. Don't touch that stick! It is a sword."

"Of course it is." She let it drop. "Nothing is as it seems. Let me tell you about Rosedene. Perhaps you can spot something that I have missed."

"May I continue working? I promise you I am listening," he said. He was sanding down a long wooden box that was set up on a pair of trestles.

"Go ahead. It soothes me to watch others labour."

"Ha, ha."

She laid out the whole business to him, point by point. He was impressed by Tobias's rat-scarer. "And it actually worked? Does the boy need a position?"

"As apprentice to you? Don't be silly, Simeon, you can

barely keep yourself in bread and coffee. Every time I come here, I expect to find you evicted and a family of Italian jewellery-makers here in your place."

"Aha," he said, flourishing a cloth and beginning to polish the smooth box. "Now you may laugh on the other side of your face, for I have changed! You are too rude to not ask how I am."

"Oh, Simeon. Please tell me: how are you?"

"Well, since you ask," he said, dripping with heavy sarcasm, "with such concern and genuine interest in my life…"

"Tell me, or I shall explore the uses of this stick. Sword. Thing."

"I have taken your advice," he said, finally ceasing his perpetual motion, and standing quite still. He gazed above Marianne's head as he spoke, like he was uncomfortable meeting her eye. "You have told me for a long time that my talents do not lie as a performer on the stage. I have been unwilling to accept that."

"I know," she said gently. "And I don't say that your talents lie elsewhere, exactly. Just that your performance needs adjustment."

"You once said that I was better as scenery."

"I might have done, but was I drunk?"

"Yes, and *in vino veritas*. But look, Marianne, look at this!" He gestured to the box that lay before him. "I have undertaken a commission for someone else. This is not for my own tricks. This is for the Marvellous Brothers Clay, and their magic show. What do you think? They are paying me handsomely for this contraption."

She got up to examine it. "It is just a box. But I am sure that it is far more than it seems. Are there sliding panels? Mirrors?"

"Both, and more besides. I am honestly rather surprised at how much they are paying me."

"You are worth it!" she exclaimed in pride. "Well done. You shall surely get as much satisfaction from seeing this in action as being on stage yourself. Um … what *does* it do?"

"The woman gets in, and she disappears! I cannot show you the mechanism while it stands on the trestles. It must be on the floor. But this panel here moves on these runners, and this side is completely false – do you see?"

She tried to follow the action of the box's sides but she could not completely picture it. "I look forward to seeing it for real," she said. "Now, then. How would you recreate ghostly screaming?"

"There is much that does not make sense in what you told me," he said. "The screams come once a night, and not every night, and not on a schedule. They cannot be traced to one source. They have no purpose. They are recent. They might be an accidental offshoot of the child's pranks but how? And why at night? And from where? I would like to see the place myself."

"I don't think it is possible," she said. "I doubt I shall ever be able to go back. It is all over, and I have failed. What a mess."

"Don't worry," he told her, in an annoying but touching role reversal. "Stay strong, and I am sure everything will be all right. I know you. You will go to bed, and wake up the next morning full of ideas. Some of them might even be the right sort of ideas."

"You are too kind."

***

It was mid-afternoon when Marianne returned home to Woodfurlong. She slipped straight to the Garden Wing, and this time was successful in avoiding being seen by Mrs Davenport. She passed by her father's room and poked her head in.

He was sitting in his favourite armchair in a pool of sunlight, his head back, and his eyes closed. He had lost more hair lately, she noticed. His nurse, the ancient and formidable Mrs Crouch, sat on a harsh upright chair with some mending in her lap. She nodded at Marianne, but pursed her lips, indicating silence. Marianne withdrew.

She changed her clothes and sat down at her desk. She had a small day room to herself, which doubled as a study, and alongside that was a shared laboratory. Truly, she was blessed in what she had been allowed at Woodfurlong, and she was ungrateful to chafe at living in someone else's house. She had more here than she could ever afford on her own.

She smiled then, at her own shortcomings. I am far too independent for Mrs Davenport to be able to succeed in her machinations, she thought, and she allowed herself a little bit of glee at that. But only a little. Now she had an unpleasant task to perform, and she could put it off no longer. She pulled her writing set open and took out a narrow-nib pen, and some good laid paper, and set to work on a letter to Inspector Gladstone that detailed every inch of her recent failure.

Once it was written and dry, she folded it carefully in the old-fashioned way she had been taught at school, so that it became its own enclosure and she didn't need one of the new envelopes, and laid it to one side.

She didn't feel ready to send it yet.

As she sat in contemplation of events, gazing out of the window rather than look at the horrible white paper evidence of her defeat, someone knocked at her door. She twisted around as Phoebe came in before Marianne had even said she might enter.

Phoebe closed the door and hurried right over to Marianne's side, agitation showing in every line of her.

"What is it?" Marianne asked in alarm, urging her to sit down. Phoebe drew up a chair and took Marianne's hands in her own. She squeezed too hard.

"My dear cuz, I implore you, I beseech you; I need your help!"

"I told you, I am not going to poison your mother," Marianne said. "Not fatally, anyway. Although I suppose it is true when they say that poisons and medicines differ only in degree."

"Oh, goodness, could you? Well. Actually, no, it was not that which I came to ask you, but it's worth knowing."

"Forget I mentioned it."

"No, no. I never forget anything of such usefulness."

As the leading gossip-merchant in the area, such a skill had served Phoebe well over the years.

"So what can I help you with? I am having no luck with screaming," Marianne said.

"I can scream, and frankly, I have been doing so every night, into my pillow," Phoebe replied. "And once, today, in the middle of the morning, when I had to turn around and stuff my face into the curtains in the drawing room. It is on account of my mother, of course." She sighed heavily. "Marianne, could you possibly advance me a small loan?"

It was the very last thing that Marianne could do. She had gathered together a small amount of money which she guarded jealously. It was to be her ticket out of Woodfurlong and into a place of her own. "How much?" she asked cautiously.

"Not so very much. It is just that before my mother arrived, I had already asked for a new gown to be made up for me, in the latest fashions, for the winter season, and some gloves of course, for they simply don't last, and a fur muff, as Mrs Cogwell said that the onions had such thick skins this year and that means a hard winter, does it not?"

"What of your allowance from your husband?"

"Price is too far under the sway of my mother," she said bitterly. "He defers to her in all things, saying her age gives her wisdom. And *she* says that I must learn to adapt my own dresses, and that I am giving society the impression that I am nothing better than an ill-bred hoyden. She told me I might as well paint my face."

"You do paint your face."

"Yes, but I do it so that it looks as if I have not. It is better that way."

"Phoebe, do you really need a new dress?"

"I do," she said, pouting. "And as I had ordered it before she arrived, I must honour my commitment. I cannot cancel.

You do not understand. My mother does not understand. She is stuck in the past. It is true that people look to me to set an example, but they want me to show taste and wealth. My mother thinks people want me to show restraint but it simply isn't true. Think of how small, and mean, and awful so many people's lives are! I bring joy and hope if I am dressed well. Are women not supposed to be a delight for the eyes?"

"I agree with your mother, to be honest. We are supposed to be *useful*," Marianne said.

"It is only a loan. Once she goes home, Price will loosen the purse strings once more. I shall pay you back with interest," she added. "Enough to make it worth your while."

"Usury, as well as pride and vanity," Marianne said. "Not to mention the duplicity of going behind your mother's back."

"When did you become such a lover of scripture?"

Marianne pulled her hands free of Phoebe's grasp, and rubbed at her temples. She could not really refuse. She paid no rent, and did not contribute to the food or general household budget. Mrs Crouch was paid for by Price, too. Marianne's earnings bought her medicines, clothing, travel, and the rest was saved, stored away for the future.

"Very well, then. Of course I will help you."

Phoebe clapped her hands. "Thank you, dear, dear cuz! You have positively saved me."

Marianne took some money from her locked box.

"Good. Now go away before I change my mind."

Phoebe danced to the door, clutching the little purse to her chest. "One more thing that you might do for me…" she said lightly.

"I've said no, about the poison."

"No, not that, not yet. You must attend dinner tonight. You have missed too many meals and I am feeling the strain of making correct conversation with my mother."

"And you think I can converse any better?"

"No, but listening to you try so hard to be good will amuse me."

"I shall bring my father, too, and then you'll be sorry." Russell rarely dined with the family.

"I know that you dare not." Phoebe pulled an inelegant face, and was gone.

***

Marianne was disturbed a little while later by another knock on her door. This time it was Mrs Crouch, telling her she was having to leave early, and would Marianne sit with her father? He was asking for her. She dismissed Mrs Crouch – as if she had any say over the nurse's movements, who would simply do as she pleased anyway – and went to talk with her father.

He was making sense, but he was tired. He asked her to read to him, but he could not quite follow the thread of the novel she chose. Then she tried the letters page of the newspaper, which had more success. It usually woke him up, and got him angry, which was something. Suddenly he told her to put the paper down, and asked what she had been doing lately.

She glowed with a warm feeling of affection. His illness was affecting his brain and some days she thought that he didn't even know he had a daughter. In some of his fits, he'd called her by her mother's name, and those nights she had cried, just a little.

She seized the chance to tell him everything about the mystery at Rosedene, hoping that his old analytical reasoning would show her what she had missed.

She ran on, almost breathless in her enthusiasm to share, and was just coming to the main point about Tobias's rat-scarer when she heard him snore.

He was asleep, and probably had been for some time.

She stifled her disappointment, and went to dress for dinner.

Eight

Dinner did not improve her mood at all. Price was notably silent throughout. Phoebe and her mother were continuing a tight-lipped discussion about the way the meal was served. The Claverdon household, like most people who were of note, had moved to the modern style of *service à la russe,* which Mrs Davenport argued should make considerable economic savings. There was no need to display elaborate heaps of food laid across the table, much of which would not be eaten. The servings were brought out in careful, small portions, and given to each individual diner.

"Management and forethought," Mrs Davenport declared, "ensures that this will save you a great deal of money and food waste. To waste food, my dear girl, is a sin. And you must set an example to the lower orders, who do not appreciate the value of things unless we teach them."

"Mother, this costs us more, because of the staff we need to serve it."

"Nonsense. They must become more efficient. Your staff are numerous and idle. You have spoiled them and you are in danger of ruining their souls. In fact you can dine like this with far fewer staff than you currently have…"

The polite disagreement rumbled on through the fish course, meats, salad and ices. The cook was usually a marvel at producing tasty food but even Marianne's hunger could not persuade her to eat too much of the dry, limp slices of beef. There was a lack of seasoning, but she didn't mention it. Mrs Davenport seemed to relish the stuff. Maybe it was some kind of penance, like an edible hair shirt.

Mrs Davenport then insisted that she retire to the drawing room with Phoebe and Marianne, leaving poor Price alone with brandy and cigars. On a quiet informal night, he would usually follow them immediately, but smoking had now been banned from the drawing room as Mrs Davenport made it into a more "feminine space where we might work upon self-improvement," which meant, in practise, tedious discussions about narrow topics, and not nearly enough wine.

Marianne tried to make eye contact with Phoebe but her cousin looked away stubbornly, and anyway, what was Marianne trying to convey? Her own frustration? Phoebe would be feeling the same way. They settled themselves in the drawing room.

Mrs Davenport asked Marianne how her day had been spent. Phoebe leapt in, immediately, asking her mother for advice about suitable hairstyles, and Marianne simply stared at her own hands. Eventually Price came in, and Mrs Davenport asked him to read some quiet, sensible literature to them. It had to be something dry, clever, moral and without a whiff of scandal. Marianne was surprised that there was such a book in the house;

Mrs Davenport must have brought it with her.

She half-listened, letting her eyes close. Phoebe had now been bullied into needlepoint, and was stabbing viciously at the fabric in the frame. Marianne hoped it was some effigy of her mother, picked out in shades of blood. She herself plotted how she might remove the pages from the terrible book Price was reading, and insert something far racier. He probably wouldn't notice. He'd drone on automatically, but it would amuse Phoebe.

And at least it stopped Mrs Davenport from plaguing Marianne further and getting onto the topic of her marriage prospects. At the very first polite moment, Marianne pleaded a headache, and fled the room. At first she congratulated herself on escaping unscathed.

But then she sank onto her bed and despair threatened to creep over her once more. The night was young. She wanted to chat to Phoebe and laugh and be merry, relaxing in front of the fire. But even that had been curtailed – a fire was an extravagance on a warm autumn night! – and they were forced to wear heavy shawls and suffer a chill for the good of their souls.

No, she wouldn't despair. She'd survived worse than this. More than survived: triumphed. She would act.

Tomorrow, she resolved, in spite of lack of funds, she *was* going to go house-hunting. She did not have enough for a decent sort of house. But she could afford something, some kind of room somewhere; and anywhere was better than here.

If the place had rats, at least she knew a lad who could scare them away for her.

Marianne was usually so organised and efficient. But for the second day running, she went into town without remembering to post the letter to Inspector Gladstone. It would only come to mind once she had gone almost to the station, and it was too far to turn back. Tomorrow, she told herself. Tomorrow, I'll do it.

It irked her but she knew she was simply avoiding the main issue. She didn't want to declare herself a failure. What else could she do, though? Short of pulling up every floorboard in Rosedene, that was.

That morning had been a particular trial. Breakfast had been silent because no one had attended the early morning family prayer session that Phoebe's mother had instigated. Mrs Cogwell was threatening to leave, but Mrs Davenport had poured scorn on that suggestion, saying that the cook would find it difficult to secure a better position than at Woodfurlong – especially as she would not be given a good "character" for leaving. She had, as yet, not persuaded Price to dismiss some of the extraneous household staff but the writing seemed to be on the wall for the male servants. Either Barrington or Dry would have to go. Marianne wondered how they'd decide. Maybe they would fight for it. The image of the two stiff, starched men, stripped to their waists in a bare-knuckle boxing ring, kept her entertained for a while, until she remembered there was a very real possibility of losing one of them, and she grew sad.

And then angry.

Phoebe had tried to hide the newspapers from her, and

Marianne was instantly suspicious. She wrestled them from her cousin in the library while Mrs Davenport was downstairs somewhere, subjecting the staff to fresh terrors.

"What?" Marianne said. "Save time. Tell me the worst right now."

"It wasn't me."

"It was your mother, I know. What has she done?" But even as she asked, she knew the answer. She turned to the matrimonial columns, the lists of adverts from people seeking partners, a surprisingly well-used section of the newspaper. Due to the anonymity and the codes, she struggled to find the one that pertained to herself.

"M, not yet 30, dark, with a fine figure and an interest in self-improvement. Wishes to correspond with a gentleman with a view to matrimony. Must have own income, and be of professional standing."

"Is that me?" Marianne asked, hopefully. "Although I am not sure about the 'not yet thirty' part. I'm nowhere near thirty."

"I think maybe it is you; or no, what about this one?" Phoebe read one out. "This has your name. *Marianne, 23, tall and well-developed, keen interest in modern matters, seeking to correspond with steady, sensible older gentleman with strong moral fibre and sense of duty.*"

"Oh, that will be it. She wants someone to rule me," she said. "I will not stand for it. When is she leaving?"

"When you are married. You had better be quick about it. Choose someone old. And you do know poisons. Things might be managed, if you know what I am saying."

"Hush, Phoebe! I am going into town today."

"Why? To find a husband? Can I come?"

Marianne opened her mouth but her breath caught in her throat. She hadn't told Phoebe of her plans. "I'm going to see Simeon," she said at last.

"Oh, how lovely. I haven't seen him for a long time."

"And what about your mother?"

Phoebe's shoulders sagged. "I know, I know. I must stay here and be dutiful. Well, say hello to him from me."

Marianne folded the newspaper back into quarters, and headed out – forgetting the letter to Inspector Gladstone yet again.

***

Marianne was waylaid from all side as she moved through the teeming streets. She stopped by a seller of hot pies and bought two, and could not resist the calls of a muffin man either. And so her meagre savings slipped on through her fingers, just like water. She loaded herself up with parcels and paper bags as she pushed her way along the pavement.

"Ho! Hello, there! Miss Starr!" a man called out, and she caught sight of a frantically waving arm. It was attached to a young man called Percy, and on his other arm was a woman she had studied with, Miss Mary Sewell, aspiring thespian, committed bluestocking, and now thoroughly in love.

"Hello, you two," she said. She attempted to embrace Mary and they laughed as the pies were squashed. "So, what is new?"

"I was going to ask you that, Marianne, you disappointment!

I have been hearing all about you, everywhere I go."

"Oh, those blasted marriage adverts? They are not of my doing, I can assure you. And anyway, you are in no position to judge another woman's choices," she added, looking at Percy. Mary had once vowed to never even look in a man's direction.

Mary's rosebud mouth fell open. "What marriage advertisements? Oh, Marianne!"

Marianne waved the idea away and dropped a pie. Percy gallantly scooped it up for her, and refolded the paper over it, tightly. "It is no matter. A misunderstanding, that is all. What are you referring to?"

"Louisa Newman," said Mary. "Is she lying? She seems honest and without guile, but I can hardly believe what she is saying, and of course, she is not well known around here; what is her past?"

Marianne gripped her parcels tightly and drew herself up, ready to go out ono a hunt if necessary. "Her past is murky. What is she saying?" she demanded. "When have you met her?"

"She was at a public talk given by that lady author, Mrs Juniper, and afterward she quite held court. Everyone listened to her. She said that *you* had declared that the only explanation for the manifestations at Rosedene could be ghosts!"

"I have said nothing of the sort. What rot!"

"Then what is causing the noises and so on?"

"I don't know."

"There you are, then! She said you could find nothing, and the police could find nothing, and therefore the screaming was coming from a place far beyond human knowledge."

"Poppycock. Utter bunkum. Just because I could not explain it – and I admit it, I could not, yet – that does not mean the reason is otherworldly. Nonsense. It is like saying that we cannot explain water so it must not really exist."

"No, that does not follow at all," Mary said, who had studied natural sciences and natural philosophy just as Marianne had. "We can explain water. But if you could not explain the noise…"

"There was a boy there, who was creating things, automata in a way, and I suspect that he is behind it all. In fact, I am sure of it."

"Without proof, Marianne, there is nothing. You know the method. Prove it – or it means naught."

"I would if I could," she said. "So this talk is all over town, is it? Spread by Mrs Newman herself?"

"Indeed so. I could hardly believe it but now that I speak to you, I see that it is true."

"Please, Mary, if you have any affection left for me, do not let the rumours spread any further. It damages my professional credibility."

"Of course not, my dear. But Marianne, although I will not speak of it to anyone again, if you cannot solve it … what of your credibility then?"

"I know," she said grimly. "I know."

Nine

"Is the whole world against me?" Marianne wailed as she stood in Simeon's rooms. She had laid out the slightly-soiled pies and muffins, and he had provided hot tea and semi-clean plates. Then he had asked her a question which provoked her outcry.

"I am not against you!" Simeon said hastily. "I only ask because, well, all this was your idea in the first place."

She sank into a chair and then sprang to her feet again as she felt something shift against the small of her back. "No, not that one," Simeon said, and steered her to a safer chair, which looked identical to the first.

"Simeon, I would love to help you, but I've just loaned money to Phoebe," she said. "And I simply must leave that house. I need what little I have left…"

"Of course, of course," he said. "Forget that I asked. I could visit the moneylenders perhaps, instead."

She felt guilt slide its tentacles around her neck. He had asked for a little money, as a loan, so that he could purchase a final few parts for the cunning box he was building.

And he was right: by building this for someone else, he was

acting on her advice that he leave the stage work to others.

"How much do you need?" she said, wearily.

He told her, adding, "It won't be for long. I shall finish it within the week, and as soon as I deliver it to them, they will pay me. They will pay me handsomely. You can still go hunting for a place to live today. You will have the money back before you sign anything."

"Oh, Simeon."

She ate the pie mechanically, and took the muffin with her to eat later. Her mouth was dry and she felt flat and defeated.

Well, she thought, as I am in this gloomy frame of mind, I might as well get everything else over with too. I cannot feel any worse, after all. She left Simeon's street and strode away.

She headed for the police station where Inspector Gladstone ruled, and decided it was now time to subject herself to his condemnation, in person rather than by letter.

But as she had not posted the letter, admitting her failure, there remained within her heavy heart one single glimmer of stubborn, determined hope.

Perhaps he would give her one final chance.

***

He did not.

In fact, he didn't give her a chance to speak at all. He met her at the front desk, and immediately drew her to a small bare office rather than his usual one, and urged her into a wooden chair. He perched on the edge of the heavy desk, and leaned forward, clasping his hands together.

"If you are here about the affair at Rosedene, I must warn you that I have some distressing news," he said. "Prepare yourself."

She knew. She knew immediately. He was using the tone of voice that people only ever used when someone had died. Her only question was, "Who?"

"Miss Dorothea Newman has died," he said.

"Oh, goodness." She nodded her head and let it sink in for a respectful moment. Then she said, "She was an old lady, of course. I hope that she rests in peace."

There was something off in Inspector Gladstone's face. He pressed his lips together like he was trying not to say something. She wanted to know what he wasn't telling her. "How did she die?" she asked, lightly.

He sat up straight. "Why would you not assume it was natural causes?"

"Because of your face. You are as clear as a telegraph."

"Hmm. Well, then. I should have you here interviewing suspects and reading their phrenology for the truth. She was suffocated."

"Good Lord! With what? A pillow? Oh, forgive my indecorous questions. I ask only as a scientist."

He lifted one eyebrow. "And I read you, too, and your curiosity is not only as a scientist. But still, I will tell you. She had a bag of sand that was heated in the kitchen and placed in her bed, of a night, to keep her feet warm."

"They used that to do the evil deed? Oh, the poor woman.

And who did it? You have them in custody, I suppose."

"Our investigation is ongoing."

"Inspector Gladstone!" she said, firmly. "I have been in that house – more times than you, I would wager. I have slept there and dined there. You do not have a wide choice of suspects. Three people and Miss Dorothea lived there. So, which one was it? Or is there yet another player I do not know about? Or even a passing house-breaker?"

"We are inclining to think it was, indeed, a random passing act by a thief who might have broken in," he told her. "Such a physical act of murder is not a woman's way; you ladies tend more to poison and so on, so that rules out both Mrs Newman the younger, and Mrs Peck the housekeeper. As for the boy that lives there, he is young, weak, and a good middle class boy with a solid education. It is deeply unlikely to have been him."

Marianne had to bow her head to bite back her sceptical laughter. All of those suppositions were nonsense, to her. If she had to kill someone, and the only method to hand was a bag of sand, why: she'd certainly do it. And the boy, Tobias, was quiet and bitter. She saw no reason *why* he might do it, but he ought to be considered capable.

"I must help you," she said.

Now it was his turn to splutter with laughter, and he did not hide it. He turned it into a slightly condescending smile. "Miss Starr, I do appreciate the offer but we are not quite so desperate as to…"

His smile faded.

She glared at him.

"Forgive me," he said, in a lower tone.

"Not so desperate as to employ ladies?"

"Worse," he said. "I was going to say, *scientists*."

"Oh. Ah." She gathered her thoughts. "Inspector Gladstone, something is very wrong in that house. Miss Newman tried to tell me that before she died. She said there was more than rats at large there. And what of the noises? Someone is up to something. I do not trust Mrs Newman nor Tobias Newman. Both of them are hiding something, I am sure of it. I have been there. I have seen and heard things. Mrs Newman is pleasant and warm to me. She might speak to me about matter she would hide from you. And I feel as if I have unfinished business there. Let me assist!"

"What would you do, then?" he said, folding his arms. "What would be your course of action now? Would you arrest them both?"

"I would be looking for evidence first," she said. "Even I know that. I would have to think about this."

"You do not have long. *We* do not have long. An arrest must be made to calm the public's fears. And to allay my superiors who are biting at my heels."

"I shall get to the bottom of this," she said, rising to her feet.

"Do not get in the way of any of my officers," he warned her. "Make your own enquiries if you must, but we are in charge, not you."

"I understand completely. I do have one question. Who now inherits the house?"

"As to that," he said. "I do not yet know."

***

Marianne went home. Over the next two days, she holed herself up in her study-cum-day room adjoining her bedroom, as much as she could. She went to the main meals and sat in silence, and attended the breakfast prayers, and generally tried to avoid Mrs Davenport as much as possible. When asked a question directly, she murmured a pat response that quoted as much scripture as possible, and agreed to every opinion that was put to her.

Now she sat at a wide table set in a bay window, and let the sunlight warm the skin of her face and hands. She could see Fletcher, the gardener, in the distance, taking cuttings from a bushy box hedge. So, Ann Davenport hadn't got her clutches into the outdoor staff, not yet. It would only be a matter of time before they were reduced in number, of course. She would expect the same standards of care in the garden to continue, to set an example, but she would want it to be achieved with fewer people.

Such budgetary restraint could well be pleasing to God, Marianne thought, but what of the livelihoods of those who relied on these wages? That didn't seem fair.

And I am yet another drain on this household, she realised suddenly. My father also. No wonder she wants to marry me off.

Marianne pushed her fingers through her hair and it came loose from its pins and clips. She piled up the hardware and let her curls fall free. She scratched at her scalp and thought about

86

poor Miss Dorothea Newman, dead in that gloomy house. At least her final year or two had not been alone. Until Tobias came to Rosedene, and then Mrs Newman, Miss Dorothea must have been utterly isolated. Poor woman. Did she have no other family?

Marianne grabbed her notebook and turned to the next blank page, and began to sketch out a family tree, with rough dates for the major events – Tobias's accident and loss of parents, Mrs Newman's widowing in America and subsequent return to Rosedene. And now Miss Dorothea's death. It had to all be linked but the months stretched out between each event and seemed to make no pattern.

She rested her chin on her hands and stared at the spider's web of lines until her eyes blurred, and she was jolted out of her reverie by a knocking at her door. She froze, and pretended not to be in, until she could work out who it was.

"Miss Starr?" It was Mrs Kenwigs' voice, the housekeeper. "There is a … person … here to see you."

Marianne jumped up and went to the door. A person? Not a lady, nor a gentleman. She wondered who it could be as she followed Mrs Kenwigs down the corridor to receive the visitor in the hall. They had not even been afforded the courtesy of being shown into a room.

It all made sense when she spotted Simeon. The shabby young man of uncertain parentage was hardly the sort of person that would be offered a brandy and a soft seat by the fire. And his state of distress added to the general impression of someone who was not *quite* welcome.

She rushed over to him. "What has happened? Are you

hurt? Why are you here? You could have sent a message. Simeon?"

He was upset, but he was also angry, which was a strange and unfamiliar emotion for him. He hardly knew what to do with the passionate fury. He took her hands, briefly, but dropped them straight away. He was agitated and he paced around, making a tiny circle around her as he spoke. "They have taken it! They did not pay me, they said, they said, they said to go to their address for the money and I went but they were not there, because they lied!"

"Who?"

"The Marvellous Brothers Clay. Jeremiah and Tom Clay. And now I do not have your money!"

That was a blow, but she thrust it aside. "Simeon, slow down. So, you have given them the box that you made, but they have not paid you?"

"I told you! I told you that. I finished it the day after you loaned me the money and they came for it this morning and took it and said I would get the money at their room but they were not at their room and never have been, for it was not their room. Now what do I do?"

"You go straight to the police. I will come with you."

"I cannot." He stopped and stared at her. "You know that I cannot."

He was white in the face and trembling. Marianne was pretty sure that he had no real reason to be so terrified of authority, but he harboured myriad strange paranoias, and his fear of the police was an enduring one. Such was the depth of his feeling that she was worried he would rather harm himself than subject himself to police scrutiny.

"Well, then. Tell me their address."

"It is fake! I went there, and an old lady answered. She did not know of them." He pulled out a scrap of paper and handed it over. "That is useless but you can have it. You may as well burn it and all my work along with it."

"Hush now. What else do you know of them?"

"Nothing. They are illusionists. And I spent all my money on that box, and all yours too. I shall be evicted. I shall die."

"Oh, Simeon. Wait here." She glanced down at his feet and saw, from the state of his shoes, that he had probably walked all the way to Woodfurlong. He didn't have the money for the train, which meant he probably didn't have the money for a message to be sent to her; and he wouldn't have any money for food. She dashed back to her room and unearthed her rapidly depleting purse. She could spare him a few of her remaining coins, enough to tide him over, at least.

She returned to the hall, calmed him down, made some spurious promises that she would help him – somehow – and sent him home. Then she sank down on a wooden settle against the wall in the hallway, next to a fern in a round pot, and sighed.

Ann Davenport swept past, and didn't notice her there at first. When she saw her, she gave a startled cry of pure horror.

"Mari-ANNE! Your hair."

She had been messing up her hair while she'd been deep in thought. Marianne gave it a half-hearted pat. "Apologies, madam." She thought of a few explanations but dismissed them all. She just smiled and shrugged. She was past caring what Mrs

Davenport thought of her right now.

Mrs Davenport scrunched her face up into a tight pucker for a moment then smoothed it out, and sailed up to Marianne. "I am shocked. I am disappointed. I am working hard on your behalf, and the least – the very least – you can do is to present an acceptable appearance."

"Oh, those matrimonial advertisements? I did not ask for you to place them."

"No, for your head is in the clouds. It has fallen to me to pick up the pieces, once again. After your poor mother died, who took charge of your education?"

"My father ensured I continued at school."

"Pah. He was only interested in book learning. No, your real education, as a woman of society. I took you into my home, and treated you as my own daughter. And yet here you are, throwing such kindness back into my face, and into the face of my daughter too!"

"I am doing no such thing," Marianne protested. "You have taken it upon yourself to treat me as a project, but I can assure you that I am perfectly able to direct my own life. Thank you."

"You are making a pretty mess of it, then. Here you live, alone, getting older by the day, with not even one suitor to your name and no effort to remedy that. Your father, God grant him peace, is old, mad and quite beyond help. He ought to be in an asylum. You are weak to think that you can care for him here. He should be in a better place. Are you not cruel for denying him proper treatment?"

Marianne's blood was thundering in her ears. She gripped

the edges of the settle tightly. "He has a nurse and regular visits from a doctor, and all the treatment that he requires."

Mrs Davenport shook her head. "You delude yourself. You are squatting here like leeches, draining blood, a burden on the resources of my poor dear daughter, and it is high time that someone *loved* you enough to tell you the truth, as I am doing. I speak only from a place of Christian compassion."

"Well, if this is compassion and love, I should hate to be your enemy," Marianne said hotly, leaping to her feet.

Her outburst shocked Mrs Davenport. She took a step back and said, with menace, "Then take care that you do not become so."

Mrs Davenport click-clacked away across the tiled floor. Her footsteps suddenly hushed as she hit the carpet and went up the wide stairs to the first floor. Marianne watched her go, with an unaccustomed feeling of hatred seething in her heart.

She clenched her fists, tried to calm herself down, and then gave up. Instead, she stormed back to the Garden Wing and found her father in a lucid enough state that she could tell him everything.

Absolutely everything, from the incidents at Rosedene to Simeon's loss of money to the Clay Brothers.

And he was not much help in offering insight, and just mumbled something about eggs, but at least he didn't fall asleep this time, and by the end of her tirade she felt a little – just a little – better.

But with still no clearer idea on what to do next.

Ten

Price and Phoebe were out that evening, attending a dinner party at the house of some friends, and Mrs Davenport stayed in her room, citing a "disorderly digestion". Marianne knew this was something to be laid at her own door. If only Marianne could be more biddable and agreeable, Mrs Davenport's digestion would be perfectly sound. It was entirely her fault.

But Marianne enjoyed having the whole dining room to herself, and dismissed all the staff, telling them she could serve herself if they just dumped all the courses on the table at once, which they did, after been sworn to secrecy.

I could get used to this, she thought, flicking through a book while she ate, one-handed, in a slovenly fashion. It reminded her of her student days. She had a relaxing evening in her room, reading and writing and generally idling, and woke the next day full of vigour and enthusiasm to attack all the problems face-on.

First, she would tackle the death of Miss Dorothea, and then Simeon's unfortunate encounter with the Clay Brothers, and finally her own parlous finances.

She dressed for the town, with a warm travelling cloak ready by the door, but sat at her desk with her notebooks so she could plan her day. She was interrupted rather sooner than she would have liked, by one of the maids clutching a note.

"This has just come for you, miss," Nettie said, bobbing a curtsey.

"Thank you. And no need to dip up and down like a seabird."

"Mrs Davenport has been training us, miss," she said, in a low voice. "I have to do better than the other girls. Otherwise…"

"Oh heavens. She has not set you all in competition against one another, has she?"

"Only one of us may stay."

It was to be a gladiatorial combat, then. "You ought to try to do well, but not well enough to win," Marianne told her. "For imagine what life will be like for the one that stays? If you are successful, how much work will you have to do?"

Nettie bit her lip. "I had not thought of that."

The maid darted away and Marianne read the note, sighed, and picked up her travelling cloak. She had to hurry if she was going to make it on time.

***

Messrs. Unthank, Dibbert and Gill had very fine, very old, and very brown offices in central London. Marianne had fought her way through the crowds, choosing to walk through the streets as being marginally faster than taking a cab or omnibus, although it meant she still arrived a little late, dishevelled and slightly sticky. The autumnal weather was pressing down on the city, trapping fog and smog under low cloud. Her pale grey gloves were covered in dark smuts of ash and dirt, and she could not bear to think of the state of her face. No wonder Ann Davenport habitually wore a lace veil whenever she had to venture into the city.

The offices were all panelled wood and gleaming brass. She was ushered into a small waiting room and a young clerk, oozing confidence, drew her to one side and quietly offered her his own handkerchief and a mirror before leading her into the main room.

Mr Unthank himself pulled out a chair for her. She found herself next to Inspector Gladstone, who nodded at Mr Unthank. "Thank you for waiting. Let us proceed."

"What is happening?" she hissed.

He nudged her to be quiet. She looked around. On chairs arranged in a semi-circle, she saw a few other familiar faces. Dressed all in black, in the deepest level of mourning, was a ram-rod straight woman who did not look her way, but Marianne could tell from the angle of her chin and cheek that it was Mrs Newman. Next to her was a thin young man, nervously jiggling one leg, which was obviously Tobias, and Mrs Peck was close by. There was another man, who had a clerk-like look about him and a notebook on his knee.

She realised it was the reading of the will as Mr Unthank began to speak in a rapid monotone.

It all went to Tobias.

And by all – there was a *lot*. Or there would be, once the house was sold. As Miss Dorothea had once hinted, all her fortune was tied up in bricks and mortar.

Marianne heard a strange rasping sound coming from her left. Mrs Newman was breathing heavily and clutching her chest. Mrs Peck had folded her arms and was frowning. She had been given a small amount of money in recognition of her service. Perhaps she had expected more.

But the house, and all its contents, was to be sold as soon as possible and everything was to pass to Tobias.

Mr Unthank finished, and folded the piece of paper precisely. Mrs Newman rose to her feet, squeaked, and fell to the floor in a faint.

Chairs were overturned. The clerk rushed to her side. Mrs Peck looked down at the sprawled figure, sighed, and to Marianne's astonishment, left the room abruptly. Tobias jumped back, and didn't know what to do. His pale face was strained and streaked, and he gripped the back of a wooden chair to keep his balance. Inspector Gladstone and Mr Unthank bent over the fallen figure, and the clerk rushed out and back in with some smelling salts.

"Mrs Newman? Mrs Newman? Miss Starr, help me please," Inspector Gladstone said. "Would you loosen her clothing for me, please? I do not want to be impolite."

As Marianne reached for Mrs Newman's tightly-buttoned jacket, the woman came back to consciousness again, slapping Marianne's hands away with a surprising vigour. Almost, Marianne thought, as if she had been faking the faint.

Mrs Newman was lifted up into a chair, and pestered with more salts, a glass of water, and a barrage of questions as to her state. She ignored them all, and addressed Inspector Gladstone.

"It was him! The wicked, wicked boy. Do you see, now? He must have done it!"

"Tobias, do you mean?"

"Of course! He has inherited everything. How can that be? Where is he? Come here and confess your sins, you evil child."

Tobias shook his head silently, staying behind the chair, his eyes wide with fear.

"Mrs Newman, please do not exert yourself. You have been under a lot of strain recently..." Inspector Gladstone murmured.

She was having absolutely none of it, and Marianne felt sympathy for her. "I have been widowed. I have returned to my native country, to the few scraps of family I have left. I have encountered ghosts. I have done my best to show love and mercy to a poor orphaned boy. I have tended ceaselessly to my aging aunt. She has died. And now – and now, I find my reward is to be left penniless and alone! Look to the boy. She is dead, and who has benefited? He has!" She pointed a shaking finger at Tobias. "Only him!"

"No, no," he said, thickly, trying not to cry.

"This would not be the first dreadful thing he has done. And you know what I am talking about, Miss Starr!"

All eyes turned to Marianne.

Mrs Newman pressed on. "Come and see, all of you. Come to Rosedene right now, with me, and I will show you. I will show you the death he has caused! There are corpses in the house, other corpses quite beside my poor aunt, may she rest in peace."

"Corpses?" Inspector Gladstone said, "Miss Starr? Can you vouch for any of this?"

"Er, no, I most certainly cannot."

"Come on, then!" Tobias suddenly shouted. "Come and see, then. I shall show you! I'll show you all these *corpses*."

Marianne expected a kind of pandemonium. So, too, did Mrs Newman. But Inspector Gladstone slowly stood up straight, and brushed down his clothing with exaggerated care. He nodded at Mr Unthank, and asked the quietly capable clerk to fetch them a cab that would take four people to Rosedene.

"There is no reason to hurry," he said to Marianne in a low aside as they moved through the offices to the street. "Not if they are corpses; they are hardly going to walk off, are they?"

"That's true. What do you think of Mrs Newman's claims?"

"They must be considered."

"Sir, she faked that faint."

"Are you sure?"

"I am a woman. Of course I am sure. We never *really* faint but they are jolly useful to get one's self out of a sticky situation – or, indeed, into one, if that is one's desire."

"Hmm. I will bear that in mind. But consider; it is true that she is now penniless. She will be genuinely distraught. She truly is alone here."

"No doubt."

They had to let the conversation end there, as they were wedged into a carriage brought out from a local stables, larger than the usual street cabs, and this subjected them to a slow and uncomfortable journey out to Rosedene. Mrs Peck was discovered waiting on the steps outside and she was bundled into the carriage along with everyone else. Marianne was next to Inspector Gladstone, and they sat opposite Tobias and Mrs Newman, who pressed themselves against the sides of the cab with Mrs Peck as a buffer in between them. Both Mrs Newman and Tobias looked out of their windows, and no one said a word.

I ought to throw Mrs Davenport at Mrs Newman, Marianne thought. It would be a perfect match. Mrs Davenport can find a husband for Mrs Newman. Then she will be busy, and Mrs Newman will not be poor.

She studied Tobias, and he was growing more agitated the closer that they got to Rosedene. His knee jiggled, his fingers tapped, and he gnawed at his lip. Every few moments he seemed to notice his nervous tics and would stop them, only for another to pop up in its place. As the carriage rolled up the gloomy driveway, he could handle no more.

"I am sorry," he burst out. "I only meant the one corpse. I know the one she means."

Mrs Newman gave an affected sob and dabbed at her eyes, which were perfectly dry. Marianne stared at her, hard, trying to convey to her that she *knew* Mrs Newman was pretending. But Mrs Newman met her gaze for a moment and looked away, unconcerned for Marianne's opinions.

It was Mrs Peck who had the keys to the great wooden doors of the house, and Mrs Newman had to wait to be let in, with everyone else. As soon as they were inside the cold, silent hall, Tobias headed for the stairs without looking back. He had a curious, limping gait, and hung on to the bannisters as he hauled himself up. Mrs Peck said, "I am sure you'll want refreshments," and went off to the kitchens at the back of the house, as if no one had mentioned corpses at all, and this was just some everyday sort of morning call.

"Tobias!" Mrs Newman shrieked.

He said, in a voice that shook slightly, "This is my house now," and continued on his way.

"Show us the things that you have found, if you are able, Mrs Newman," the inspector said in a kind and patient voice. Marianne looked at him and hid her smile. So, he was faking too; but then, that was part of his job.

Mrs Newman led them the way that Tobias had gone, though he was out of sight now. To Marianne's surprise they didn't stop at the first floor, but instead continued up to the attic level. They turned the corner and Mrs Newman pointed down the corridor to the shadows at the far end. "Down there!" she whispered.

"But I told you about this," Marianne said. "I explained everything."

"What?"

Gladstone walked away down the corridor, and Mrs Newman hung her head, sniffing and making little crying sounds. For a moment, Marianne wondered what was real and what was not. Her sobbing sounded pretty convincing. And she had plenty of reasons to cry.

Gladstone reached the shadows and made a startled grunt, and then said, "Well. Miss Starr, you knew about this?"

"If it is a stuffed cat, rather large, with fake green eyes, then yes, I did. I was going to tell you when I came to see you but you rather stymied me with the news of the death. Stay there." She walked forward, keeping to the edge of the corridor, feeling deliberately with each footstep until she hit the right spot and the circuit was completed. Gladstone barked out with a laugh of surprise. She stepped off the floorboard, and the glowing eyes went out again. On, and they flickered into life. He saw immediately what she was doing.

"How curious," he said. "Electrical trickery, I assume?"

"It is to scare the rats away," she told him.

"Of course, of course. And does this cause the screaming at night?"

"No. As to that, it remains a mystery."

"It could only have been ghosts," Mrs Newman said.

"Could have?" Marianne asked. "Have they not been heard recently?"

"Not since poor Dorothea died. Perhaps ... oh, it is too awful."

"Perhaps *she* was the originator of the mystery? No, I cannot see that at all," Marianne said. "And it certainly was not ghosts. You seemed convinced of that – at first."

Mrs Newman sighed in tired exasperation. "Well, whatever it was, we shall never know. I believe it was ghosts, in the end, and unless you can find evidence to the contrary, you must believe the same. My question to you, Inspector Gladstone, is this: will you ignore the terrible actions of that boy? Is a dead cat and a suspicious inheritance not enough for you?"

"It is a consideration, certainly," he said carefully. "Come, let us find these refreshments that Mrs Peck has organised for us."

There followed a most awkward quarter-hour, and Marianne thought that the meals at Woodfurlong had been excruciating enough. They were nothing compared to perching on a dusty chair in a room all covered in dustsheets, still wearing hat and gloves, sipping at too-hot tea from chipped china cups that did not match their saucers. Mrs Peck brought out some fancy biscuits, shortbread and so on, which tasted more of brick dust than anything else. Inspector Gladstone got halfway through one before laying it aside and trying unsuccessfully to hide it under a teaspoon. He addressed Mrs Newman.

"We are taking the death of your aunt very seriously," he said. "The boy has weakened limbs, and until today, he quite clearly did not know that he was the sole beneficiary of the will. There are other suspects."

"Who?" she demanded. "And he is not as weak as you think. Don't be deceived. He could be pretending to be surprised."

More fakery? Marianne thought. Who in this household is actually honest? "You once told me he was not a liar, and you thought him to be totally honest."

"Maybe he is so good at shamming that even I was deceived!" Mrs Newman snapped. "He is stronger than he looks!"

"Is he really?" Gladstone said mildly. "I shall bear it in mind. But I need to inform you that two ruffians were reported in the area, earlier that same evening. One householder caught them in his outhouse, having broken the lock on the door. He chased them off, and they are still at large. My policemen report to me that this house is not as secure as it ought to be. They have found many loose windows and points of entry."

"Oh."

"Do you see, then, that the murderer could have come from outside?"

"I do," she said, slowly, nodding. "Oh, I do see. Oh. But still: what of Tobias?"

"Well, I am not going to arrest the boy. Not yet, at any rate."

"And here he is." Mrs Newman spoke a little more kindly now, as if she had fixed only upon the idea that Tobias was guilty, and was now almost relieved to discover that someone else could have done the terrible deed.

Tobias entered the room slowly, but his eyes were fixed on the plates of food on the table.

"Here," Marianne said, thrusting some biscuits at him. "When did you last eat?"

He shook his head at the question but scooped up the nasty shortbreads and ate them quickly, staying at a distance from everyone else. Mrs Newman offered to pour him some tea, but he wouldn't look at her. He seemed to be working up to saying something. He coughed, and they all waited, looking at him.

"You have to go," he said at last.

"We are on our way," Inspector Gladstone said. "Mind that you stay here, young man. We may have more questions for you. I would advise you to engage a tradesman immediately and make the house secure. I can arrange to have one sent to you, if you like; you have a sudden burden thrust upon you. I can recommend an honest man."

"I am not scared," he replied.

"I am sure you are not. You must be a very brave boy. Mrs Newman, perhaps you could even consider taking Tobias and going to a hotel for a few days? Just tell me where you go, that is all I ask."

"No," Tobias said, firmly. "I meant, you must all go. You must leave this house. This is my house now, isn't it? So, get out.

Everyone." He was looking now at Mrs Newman. "Even you. Especially you."

"Tobias! You cannot do this."

"Tobias," Gladstone said, going up to the boy and putting his hand on his shoulder. Tobias shrugged it off. "You are, what, fifteen? You cannot stay here alone."

"I am sixteen, actually, turned just last month, and I can stay here if I want to."

"You must have a guardian of some kind, and Mrs Newman is closest to you."

"I do not need her. I do not trust her. You can all leave. She is no connection to me."

"Tobias, I have nowhere to go," Mrs Newman said.

"Find a hotel, like the man says."

Mrs Newman sobbed again, and there was definitely a note of anger, frustration and genuine sorrow in it. "Please…"

"Get out!" he roared, his voice cracking and squeaking.

Inspector Gladstone went to Mrs Newman's side but she pushed him away just as Tobias had done. She gathered up her shawl and her bag, and half-ran to the door.

"Wait," Marianne called. "Where are you going?"

But she was gone. Marianne looked at Inspector Gladstone in stunned surprise. "We should go after her."

"She will come back, surely," he said. "She will have her things here. Clothing and so on."

"I shall *not* let her in," Tobias said.

Gladstone wavered, and then went after Mrs Newman.

"Why not?" Marianne asked Tobias.

"I do not like her and she does not like me. Now you both may go. But…"

"What is it?"

"I am sorry about everything. I really am. I don't know what I should do now."

"You probably shouldn't stay here on your own. The house will be sold. Perhaps you can use the funds for continuing your education. Had you thought of a profession, perhaps?"

"No. What can I do?"

"You are talented. You are practical and clever," she said. "I admired your rat-scarer immensely. You should study natural sciences. What about your interest in electricity? It is very much the new thing and you might make your fortune in it."

"Perhaps."

She had an idea. "Look, you can certainly stay here, but I think you will be alone and miserable, and those biscuits are truly dreadful. I have a friend, a male friend, called Simeon Stainwright. He is like you, in some ways. He is a stage illusionist, and lives alone, and has space. At least consider staying with him for a few days."

"Why would he let me stay? I am a stranger to him."

"He needs the money," she said. "That is the long and short of it. At least come and meet him. You can buy some nicer food on the way. That way, it won't be a wasted journey, even if you don't stay with him."

He didn't say anything. Marianne went to the kitchens to tell Mrs Peck that everyone was leaving.

"What am I to do?"

105

"You should be looking for a new position," she said. "I am sorry."

"I am owed wages."

"Apply to Mr Unthank, perhaps?"

"And a character, to help me get a new position?"

"I am so sorry."

Mrs Peck turned away with a muffled curse, and Marianne knew she would be rifling the cupboards to take away as many saleable goods as she could. Marianne could hardly blame her.

Tobias was still waiting for her. He didn't say anything but there was a defeat in the slope of his shoulders. He trailed after her as they left the building. They found Inspector Gladstone standing forlornly on the steps by the carriage, breathing heavily and red from exertion.

"She said low things to me, and has gone," he said. "She has quite a rich vocabulary for a lady. But I marked the hotel that she has fled to, not far from here, and I spoke with the manager, who will keep me informed of her movements."

"Excellent. Let us get back to the city. Do you carry brandy on your person?" she asked as they swung up into the carriage.

"I do. Do you feel faint?" He passed her a small bottle.

"No. I wish I did; it would distract me from the taste of brick dust or whatever was in those biscuits." She sipped the fiery liquid and passed it to Tobias with a wink. He didn't smile, but he did take a drink, and after a little while, the alcohol made them relax and they rolled back into London with almost a sense of merriment in the air.

Eleven

She alighted the carriage a street away from Simeon's workshop. She had quashed her doubts with a few more sips of brandy, and ignored Tobias's growing mews of reservation and protest. She took a firm grip on the boy's elbow and steered him through the crowds. He evidently did not come into town very often, and he looked around him with wonder and excitement.

She only let go of his arm when she purchased some lukewarm meat pies from one seller, and some fresh hot bread rolls from a bakery boy who was strolling the streets with a tray around his neck. Tobias was not going to make a run for it when there was free food in the offing.

He was still eating when she reached the workshop. Tobias struggled with the rickety wooden steps because his hands were full, meaning that he couldn't drag himself up by the railings. She ran up ahead and hammered on the door.

To her relief, Simeon looked relatively calm. "Have you found it? My money?"

"I have not. But I have brought you a source of cash and even, dare I say it, companionship."

"I do not need companionship. If I did, I'd get a dog. A small, quiet one."

"He is much the same," she said, glancing down at the boy who was halfway up the steps now. "He needs somewhere to live. He's from Rosedene. It's Tobias Newman. He's lost everything, Simeon; everything except money, which he has inherited. He built the rat-scaring device that I told you about."

Simeon's eyes lit up. "Tobias! Direct current or alternating current? Which do you favour?"

Tobias got onto the platform at the top, and caught his breath. "For what purpose?" he asked.

"Lighting the city!"

"Alternating, of course."

"And the dangers?"

"Minimal. Tesla has shown us that. As long as one does not try to – I don't know, drink it – as long as one takes care, then it must be alternating current, unless we want a great power station on every street corner. Consider the dangers of gas, after all…"

Simeon grinned, and drew the boy inside, and Marianne was left staring at a suddenly closed door. At least she still had a bread roll.

So she walked, to clear her head, and then tucked herself up in a half-empty second class carriage as she took the train back to Woodfurlong. She thumbed through her notebook. Was it worth pursuing the matter of the screams at Rosedene? Undoubtedly not, except that her methodical mind could not bear the loose end.

108

What of the death of Miss Dorothea? Marianne could not now picture Tobias committing such a crime. Yes, he had inherited money, but he was thrown into chaos since his aunt's death. She had suspected the boy at first, but no longer. He had not known he would inherit.

As for Louisa Newman, she was ringing many bells of suspicion in Marianne's mind. Perhaps she had expected to inherit. Marianne played it out: yes, that made sense. If Mrs Newman thought that she would inherit Rosedene, that would give her the motive to kill Miss Dorothea and supplant her. That would also explain her shock upon learning that Tobias had inherited everything.

Suffocation, not a woman's crime, pah! She replayed Inspector Gladstone's words. What nonsense. She had half a mind to suffocate someone right before his eyes, just to prove a point.

The stuff about burglars being in the area was a mere distraction. Mrs Newman could easily have done it. Perhaps she had help in the deed. Mrs Peck, then, would be a perfect accomplice, surely?

She had to convince Inspector Gladstone to question Mrs Newman more closely. He had accepted Marianne as a lady scientist; he had to accept another woman as a potential suffocator.

And if he would not, then she would do the work for him. She should have asked him which hotel Mrs Newman had fled to. No matter, she thought. She would get home and send a message out to the police station. She was likely to get a reply within the day, depending on which of the many daily postal deliveries she was able to catch; out at Woodfurlong they had only six, but in the city, letters would arrive a dozen times a day.

If she did not hear from him by the following morning, well, she'd simply travel to Rosedene and hunt for every hotel in the vicinity, and find Louisa Newman that way. It would be simple. There would not be many to choose from.

She would have made more detailed plans beyond that, but the train was pulling into the station and she needed to alight without dropping her notebook, losing her gloves, knocking her bonnet off, stepping on other people's toes, and all the usual kerfuffle of a railway.

She did take time to think about *how* she would question Mrs Newman. As Marianne walked back to Woodfurlong, she considered what her aim was. Mrs Newman was sure to suspect Marianne for working with the police, and therefore Marianne could not hope to befriend her and trick a confession out of her.

Evidence was not going to be present, either. The police would have sent their own men all over Rosedene. Marianne wondered, then, who they were, and how she might get to talk to them. *They* were the ones to befriend, perhaps. A man of science or medicine allied to the police would be a very good person to know.

She would have to be honest with Mrs Newman. Blatantly so – bullyingly so, perhaps. Marianne bit her lip as she walked. Could she do that? Should she do that? Would she not be better off behind the scenes, investigating quietly, rather than challenging suspects openly?

Doubt invaded her. Her stomach flipped. She blundered into Woodfurlong, almost in a daze, as too many possibilities, and possibilities of embarrassing failure, flashed before her eyes.

Then she stopped dead. There was a way of approaching Mrs Newman as a representative of the police *and* not arousing her suspicion, all at the same time. Yes. *Yes!* She had it. She could do this.

She ignored the approach of Mrs Kenwigs, and waved at her as she strode past, heading for the Garden Wing.

"But Miss Starr – I must tell you, your father…" Mrs Kenwigs said desperately.

"Thank you. I shall see to it."

She didn't think anything would be seriously wrong. She went first to her own room and dumped her bag on her bed. She was just stripping off her gloves, and untying the ribbon of her bonnet, when Mrs Crouch knocked at her door and came in.

"He is gone," the nurse announced. She didn't bother with polite formalities. She had spent years performing some of the most unpleasant tasks a human ever had to do for another human being, and saw that everyone was the same, underneath. She had an egalitarian, Quakerish way of dealing with people. "He has dressed for going out, and taken his good cane, but I don't know where he has gone, or when he went, or how. Daft old bugger."

Marianne dropped her bonnet onto the bed. "Oh, for goodness' sake, really? Had he said anything about going anywhere?"

"Like I say, nothing. No clue."

"There must be some clue." Marianne followed Mrs Crouch

111

to her father's day room, and looked around. "There will be a newspaper, open at an advertisement which has caught his eye – he might have gone to a druggist's shop to buy some new cure. There will be a notice, perhaps of a scientific lecture, and he will try to attend it. There will be *something*."

"You're spending too much time with the police," Mrs Crouch said. "Clues don't exist in real life. Things either are, or they aren't."

Marianne gazed around. The room was in comfortable disarray, with books and leaflets and pamphlets and notebooks all over the place. Cushions were piled up on the chairs and couches. He had a set of reading glasses on every table, and though Mrs Crouch tried to keep his potions and medicines all in one place, he was inclined to pick up bottles and leave them lying around in places that they ought not to be. Marianne spotted one wide-necked brown bottle peeking out from behind a plaster bust of Aristotle on the mantelpiece. She picked it up and shook it. Empty, but it had once contained Calomel.

Mrs Crouch sniffed, and took the bottle from her. She bustled out of the room, collecting other poisonous detritus as she went.

Marianne had to admit that there were no obvious clues, and it was frustrating that no one could say how long he'd been absent. She wandered through to the shared laboratory, and ran her hands along the wooden bench. Unfortunately her skin snagged on something sticky and she recoiled, and ran to a basin to rinse the substance off. It didn't smell but there was no telling what it was.

What experiments had her once-famous chemist father been performing lately? Sometimes he seemed to simply mix things together just to see if they exploded. In his heyday, he had been a model of precision and method. Now, it was as if he were challenging God, cooking up volatile substances, almost asking to be blown to smithereens.

There was no apparatus set up except her own little Voltaic pile where she'd been playing around with magnets. She paced up and down, and threw open a window to let in some fresher air. As she did so, she spotted a leather pouch amongst other clutter on the windowsill, resting on the top of a pile of books, and next to a top hat and a clockwork duck.

She picked it up and peered inside as she walked across the laboratory. Her father's medicines came in an assortment of containers, depending on the materials they reacted with, and she was curious to discover what the pouch contained. It was a white powdery substance. She sniffed it carefully but it was completely odourless. She decided against tasting it, and instead put it down on the bench close to the door.

She left the laboratory by the door to the main corridor and heard rushing footsteps approaching from the central part of the house. She was relieved to see it was her father, and alarmed to see that he was running.

"Father! Slow down."

"I need weapons!"

"What?" She tried to grab his arm but he was strong and pushed her against the wall. She screamed, hamming it up to appeal to his paternal sense, but he didn't even seem to notice he'd just hurled his daughter into a solid object. He ran to his room and slammed the door behind him.

Her heart was hammering now. She shot after him and grabbed the door handle, but he had already locked it. She thumped her fists on the door. "Open up! Or I shall have the door broken down! What is wrong? Are you in danger? Are *we* in danger?"

He yelled back at her, and his voice sounded very close to the door. "I shall *not* open up, and you will have the decency to afford your poor, ailing father some privacy. Nothing is wrong. We are not in danger. Go away. Bring me coffee."

"Why do you need weapons?"

"I … need coffee," he said. "That is all. I am helping you, you silly girl, so you ought to help me. Coffee. See to it, or do you have another use that I don't know about?"

She stepped away from the door. Mrs Crouch had appeared and had folded her arms, with a sour expression on her face as if Marianne's father's vagaries were somehow the daughter's fault.

"He would like some coffee," Marianne said.

"So I heard," Mrs Crouch replied. And she turned around and headed back for the day room.

Marianne sighed and went off to the kitchens, wondering if she was even going to be able to procure anything at all, now that the larders were under strict lock and key.

***

Such was the lot of an unmarried and rapidly aging – well,

114

mid-twenties – woman, Marianne thought, as she dealt with a dozen little issues and none of them were her own. She could not get coffee from Mrs Cogwell but Mr Barrington beckoned her into his own little cubbyhole and revealed a private stock in a small tin. She took some in exchange for promising to put in a good word about him to Mrs Davenport, who had not yet exercised her ruthless pruning of the staff. Instead, she seemed to be enjoying the game of pitting them all against one another. Certainly, the household was running like clockwork now, as they all desperately tried to prove their worth.

Marianne helped the children's nurse carry some coals upstairs, as the youngest child, little Charlie, had developed a chill. Ann Davenport had the cause down as a result of bad air in the nursery but Marianne thought it was his bland diet of potatoes that probably didn't help. There was a sulphurous smell all through the upper floors, as if someone had been purifying something, and the maids had opened all the windows to try to shift it.

Finally she was able to send her note to Inspector Gladstone, asking for the name of the hotel, and sent it away with the mid-afternoon post.

She was not able to come up with an acceptable excuse to release her from that evening's meal. And to her horror, a few local people "of the right sort" had been invited around to take drinks and make conversation after the dinner, although they were not invited to partake in the food itself. Marianne dragged herself reluctantly into the drawing room and installed herself in a corner, hidden as much as possible by a large fern in a pot.

Phoebe spotted her immediately and sidled over, bringing wine.

It was well watered-down. She was going to have to drink an awful lot of it for there to be any effect.

"So, these people are good enough to be entertained, but not quite good enough to be fed?" Marianne said in a low voice.

"It is my mother's doing. Apparently it is a perfectly acceptable practice and she thinks her economy is being applauded all over town."

"And is it?"

"No," Phoebe said with a grim laugh. "We are now known as the haunt of misers, and I think people have only accepted tonight's invitation so they might discover the depths to which we have sunk. She must go, Marianne. If you will not lightly poison her, I shall. Tell me what to us. And if you won't tell me, I'll go straight out tomorrow and buy arsenic fly papers. How many will I need?"

"She will only leave when she has thoroughly destroyed everything," Marianne said.

"You mean, when she has married you off. Why not consider it? I have had the most marvellous idea, Marianne." Phoebe's eyes glittered and Marianne wondered if her cousin had turned to laudanum lately. "Why not marry Simeon? Just for a while."

"You cannot marry someone temporarily."

"Oh, divorce is easier now, as long as he will agree to it. Anyway, you don't even need to divorce, if you have no intention of marrying properly. Just marry him, make her happy, she will leave and then we can carry on with our lives."

"That is ridiculous," Marianne said. "Oh, keep smiling. Someone is coming with a most determined air. Who is this?"

"One of your potential suitors. Think, Marianne. Look at his teeth! Could you bear to look at them every day of your life? Goodness me, they are almost looking back at us. If you cannot face that sight, consider my plan."

The middle-aged man bore down on them, smiling with a mouthful of grey gravestones crowding his thin-lipped mouth. Phoebe made the introduction and left Marianne to converse about beef cattle for a very long fifteen minutes. By the end of it, she was seriously considering the merits of Phoebe's suggestion. A little light poisoning would be easy enough.

And the night was yet young.

Twelve

The reply from Inspector Gladstone came to Marianne the next morning, and she headed out without seeing anyone, although as it was such a large household, she knew that she herself would have been seen. The servants were becoming more and more invisible as they sought to stay out of Mrs Davenport's way. She wanted them to be efficient, but they were to do so in a completely anonymous manner. She only used their surnames, and hardly addressed any of them directly, unless she was criticising them.

For such a Christian woman, Marianne thought, she certainly didn't see any spark of the Holy Spirit in anyone else. For Ann Davenport, the world was as it was due to God's influence and nothing more. No one had any control over their station in life, and it was simply their duty to accept it. That morning, after breakfast, Mrs Davenport had cornered Marianne and told her, in detail, of her personal sorrow at being such an exalted woman – "For it puts me under such pressure to live up to the station into which I have been born, and yet, though it pains me, do I shirk it? No! I delight in the labour, as should you…" and so on.

It was a relief to Marianne to be in motion again, travelling by train and by foot, though the constant journeys were depleting her meagre funds even more. She'd be travelling third class, at this rate, soon. Then Mrs Davenport would never find a suitable husband for her.

She had the name of the hotel, but not the address. So much for the helpfulness of the London policeman. She should have been more explicit in her note. She found the hotel after asking three boys. The first two lied, and she was sent down random alleys, but the third was an honest sort who took her right to the door and was rewarded with a shiny coin that would be good for at least a loaf of bread.

It was a small, cheap and shabby place. That told Marianne that Mrs Newman really was lacking in funds. Well, she thought, there we have something in common. Perhaps we can bond over our shared poverty. She went over her plan in her head, and prepared herself for the line she was going to take. When she was ready, she asked the smartly-uniformed man in the front lobby where she might find Mrs Newman, and he shook his head sadly.

"She's gone, madam."

"When did she leave? How long did she stay for?"

"One night only, and she went before breakfast."

"Do you know where she went?"

The man grinned ruefully, and nodded at a door that led to a small office. "We have no idea, but if you find out, do let us know, for she owes money for that night and my boss is hopping mad about it. She sounded like she could pay, you know. She sounded like a lady."

"I don't suppose she left anything in her room?"

He laughed. "Left? She arrived with nothing. I half think she might have left with more. We've not counted the silverware yet."

"Ah – you probably should."

"We don't actually have any."

She trudged out onto the street again. A chill wind was blowing. This was a quiet part of town, though the road was busy with through traffic heading into London with goods to sell. There were few shops or businesses. She walked the few streets back to Rosedene, and went up the driveway and around the cypress hedge. Now she was hidden from the street, and she stopped, staring up at the blank-faced house.

The curtains were all drawn across the windows, though she waited, expecting something to flutter and part and reveal a ghostly face. Of course, that didn't happen. The ground floor windows had been partly boarded over. She wondered if that was Inspector Gladstone's doing, or the work of the solicitors' firm dealing with Miss Dorothea's will. She tried the front door, but it was locked, as she had expected. She stepped back again, trying to see something, anything, which might give her a clue as to its secrets.

What would Louisa Newman do? She'd come back, of course, Marianne reasoned. She had left carrying nothing, so this place must still contain her clothes and personal effects. Marianne trudged around the house. There was a flagstone path that hugged the side of the house, slimy with moss, and she followed it, trying every window and door that she came across. The windows at the side and back had not been boarded over, but all were firmly locked. She remembered what Inspector Gladstone had said about the windows being old, with inefficient locks, and tried to prise some of them open, but she could not.

She was carrying her usual lock-picking equipment, and she decided to try her luck on the kitchen door. She knelt down, bunching up her skirts to pad her knees, and probed into the lock. This was an easy task on a simple internal door, but this one frustrated her. She sent a bent wire in, feeling for the wards that she could push up in the right sequence, but there were no satisfying clicks telling her she was on the right track.

It was a tumbler lock, with moving pins, quite modern and most infuriating. She would need to pass a number of bent wires in, and hold them in place as she worked. She gave up, and sat back, shoving her tools back into her bag in exasperation. She was out of practice.

She continued on, and found no obvious place that Mrs Newman could have gained entry to the house.

Her great plan to cunningly interview the woman and unravel the murder of Miss Dorothea was not going to work.

She walked to the train station, ignoring the stares of passers-by, who were curious about the large damp stain on the front of her skirts. Where would Louisa Newman go? Who else did she know in London, or indeed, Britain? She remembered that Mary had met her, but that had been in a public gathering.

Only Tobias could help her now.

She decided she would change her clothes, grab some food if possible, check on her father, and head out later to Simeon's to talk to the boy. Her father's recent antics had concerned her, and she wanted to reassure herself that he was all right.

As soon as she stepped into Woodfurlong, she was set upon by Ann Davenport, and all her plans fell into dust.

Again.

***

"Marianne! You must change at once. I shall send that girl de Souza to assist you," Mrs Davenport announced, bearing down upon her. She stopped halfway down the flight of stairs and looked up at the balcony. "Yes, Phoebe, yes. Send your girl to Marianne."

"I do not need any help, but thank you."

"You do. You must be ready within the hour. Four distinguished gentlemen dine with us tonight, and I have invited them to make polite conversation in the parlour beforehand. Two will be arriving early. It is unusual but I wish you to make their acquaintance. They should see you in a natural light. Wear a pale blue, if you will. Anything else will seem coquettish."

Phoebe leaned over the railing. "She has never been coquettish in her life. She could dress as a Parisian dancing girl and still seem as dull as a railway timetable."

"Railway timetables are not dull," Marianne shot back. "They are full of the promise of travel and adventure. Also, I do not think I have a blue dress."

Mrs Davenport threw up her hands. "De Souza!"

Phoebe was still watching. She mouthed, from behind her mother's back, "Please," and there was a look of desperation in her eyes.

"Very well." Marianne stamped off to her rooms, followed by Emilia de Souza, who was usually Phoebe's lady's maid. "Do you think she'll let me wear green? That's all I have. Look."

"It is an unlucky colour," Emilia commented. She was a quick-witted young woman, deft with her hands and discreet with her manner. "There is too much of a hint of the faeries about it."

"I thought it was unlucky due to arsenic," Marianne said.

"That too. But it was always a bad colour to wear. Why would they even make a dress like this?" Emilia sighed, and spread out the offending article on the bed. "But it is the only thing in a style that will please Mrs Davenport, so it will have to do."

"How are you faring with Mrs Davenport? Has she threatened you at all?"

"She does not like my name."

"She calls you by your surname, I noticed."

"She thinks both my Christian name and family name are too high for a woman like myself. If she had her way, all the maids here would be called Mary. But do not fear. I am in no danger from her."

Thirty minutes later, and Marianne said, "Emilia, you are a true treasure. A wonder of the world. I almost look presentable!"

Emilia stepped back and smiled wryly. "Mrs Davenport has

124

requested that you are to be made to look *marriageable*."

"Oh. That might be a task too far, even for you."

"I have done my best. Mrs Claverdon says that you are to choose one of the men tonight."

"Did she say it in a commanding sort of way?"

"Despairing. She is not happy about the whole thing. But she has confided in me, and it may be the better option. For us all."

"Do you know anything of the men that are being thrust upon me tonight?" Marianne asked.

"I have heard only of one of them. Mr William Thorne."

"Can you tell me about him?"

Emilia raised one delicate eyebrow. "If I am only to speak well of people, then no, I cannot."

"Oh, that does not sound promising. Ugh." Marianne straightened up and smoothed down her dress. Someone knocked at the door.

"Yes, yes, I am on my way!" she said. "Thank you, Emilia. You may go."

Emilia left and Mrs Crouch took the chance to come in.

"He's gone again."

Her fears flared up once more.

Thirteen

Unfortunately, there was nothing that Marianne could do about her father's wanderings. She had never discovered where he had gone on the previous time he had escaped. He was a grown man and she could hardly call the police about it. Much as she wanted to go out in pursuit of him, she had no idea where to start. Nor did Mrs Crouch.

They held a hurried conference. In the end, the severe Mrs Crouch actually demonstrated some sympathy. "I am sorry, lass. But he came home before and he will come home again. He was lucid today, you know. I think he just chafes at being here. He calls me his jailor and then blames his outbursts on his medicines, which is not true."

"He's just running off to prove a point?"

"Grasping freedom, I think. A little bit of spite, too."

Marianne wanted Mrs Crouch to give her a hug but the nurse just sighed, smoothed down her hair with a flick of her wrist, and said, "I will tidy up and go home. Unless there is anything else…?"

"No, no. Thank you for everything."

Marianne calmed herself down. Her father did sometimes visit London but he had never done so secretly before – that was the problem, in Marianne's eyes. But his nurse was right. And there was nothing she could do.

She went into the parlour with her head held high, and looked around with as much of a supercilious air as she could manage. If none of the men actually *wanted* to marry her, then there was nothing to do done, surely? She wondered how to make herself thoroughly unpleasant without angering Mrs Davenport.

She was introduced to Mr Thorne, who turned out to be a jolly man, tall and dark, with a deep and throaty laugh. In fact she never once saw any other emotion but mirth on his face, and after a while began to suspect it was chemically induced.

Perhaps she could ask what he was imbibing, and procure some for her father. Or herself.

The other guests arrived slowly; Mr Tipton, Mr Bannerjee, and Mr Smith, who was as forgettable as his name. Only Mr Tipton held any attraction for her, and that was slight.

There were a few others, too, otherwise it would have looked far too much like an auction of Marianne's spinsterhood. The dinner party had been put together with only a few weeks' notice – Mrs Davenport must have planned it from the very beginning. So there were Mr and Mrs Jenkins, who turned up to most things, and the vicar and his wife, the Forsters.

It was the first time that Marianne had seen Price Claverdon for a few days, except at silent breakfasts. He looked pained. Clearly, the issues of household economy were wearing on him, too. And he didn't feel as if he had the authority to tell his wife's mother to leave, according to Phoebe.

Ha, Marianne thought. And we're the weaker sex who supposedly can't suffocate an old lady to death?

There were fifteen minutes to wait until they were to be called into the dining room. Marianne was clock-watching as she politely listened to Mr Smith tell her all about the manufacture of cotton cloth. At least once they were at the table, she would have something else to occupy herself with. She itched to be away from this place, tracking down Louisa Newman, and avenging Miss Dorothea. And finding her father, as well. He had to be home before midnight, surely.

"Mm – are you expecting another guest?" Mr Smith asked.

"What? Oh. No. Sorry. You were telling me of the terrible effect the labour laws are having on your productivity..." she said, feeling absolutely no sympathy at all for the man and his overworked factory staff, especially the children.

"You are glancing to the door."

"I ... am sorry. I suffer from various disorders and complaints," she said. "One of them means I often have to dart away and attend to ... my ailment. This has led me to be constantly aware of my exits. I am sure you understand." She smiled sweetly and watched his imagination come up with a dozen different things that she might be alluding to. None were pleasant, judging by the creases on his cheeks as his mouth pulled down.

Good, she thought. He will hardly propose to me now.

The little knot of people standing by the door suddenly all turned, as one, to face it. Marianne craned her neck to see what the matter was. Mr Smith stood up, and put one hand out to Marianne, as if to stop her, so she immediately stood up as well.

129

"Miss Starr, please. There is a ruffian outside, shouting."

"Excellent." A distraction, she thought. She went towards the consternation. The door to the hallway was now open, and Mr Barrington was trying to calm down a wild, arm-flailing figure. The house steward spotted Marianne and jerked his head. "It's your friend again. Bit of a habit, this."

Mrs Davenport caught Marianne's arm as she headed towards the little scene at the bottom of the stairs.

"You must let me go!" Marianne said. "He is no ruffian. That's my friend, Simeon. He has been here before."

"He is quite clearly not an appropriate acquaintance and must be dropped immediately." Mrs Davenport looked back into the room. "Do any of you gentleman have a firearm?"

"No one is to shoot Simeon! Don't be ridiculous." Marianne shook herself free and raced over to her friend. He was dressed in trousers that didn't match his oversized suit jacket, with his yellowing shirt untucked and his hair wild about his eyes. "Come away. Let us talk outside."

"Marianne!" Mrs Davenport commanded. "Come back here."

She ignored it; she was not a dog to be ordered about like that. Marianne got hold of Simeon's arm and Mr Barrington hauled on the other, and together they half-lifted him out of the house and onto the front steps. It was already getting dark. "Thank you, Mr Barrington."

"A pleasure, miss. I fear you might be in trouble, however."

"Perhaps so, but it will give you all something to gossip about."

He almost smiled. "We have enough of our own problems."

130

"I know. But I am going to do my best to solve them. There is one way out of this."

"Don't marry any of them. Not on our behalf. We've been talking, you know." Mr Barrington hesitated as he was about to leave them on the step. "Please, miss. Consider your own happiness. She can't stay here forever." He dropped his voice. "And you know about poisons…"

"Not you, too! I shall pretend I did not hear that."

He slipped away inside. She heard shouting and some hysterical crying, abruptly cut off when the heavy door slammed shut.

"Now, Simeon, what is all this about? And thank you, by the way, from saving me from an interminable evening of potential marriage proposals."

"You won't be thanking me in a moment, when you hear why I am here."

"Tell me. Honestly, it cannot be worse than marriage to Mr Smith and his factory full of child slaves. Is it Tobias? Is he all right?"

"He is fine. No, it is much worse. I am here concerning your father."

"Oh God. My father is always concerning. What has he done? Is he at your place? Thank goodness."

"He was but he is not there now. He came to see me, demanding to know the details of the Clay Brothers. How did he even know about that?"

"I told him. I didn't think he was listening, to be honest."

Simeon picked compulsively at his fingernails and pulled a long strip of skin away from the side of his thumb. "He shook me."

"I know he can be overbearing."

"No, I mean, he picked me up and shook me. Physically shook me. My teeth rattled. I have bruises. He is strong. Tobias went to hide in a cabinet and got himself stuck. I don't think he was expecting the false back to pop open."

"But what of my father?"

"He wanted to know all the details so he could find them. The brothers. I told them the address was fake, and he got very angry and said he was going to use his contacts to track them down. He said he had to make things right."

"But why you? Why is he doing this at all?"

"I don't know!"

"And what about Tobias?"

Simeon clapped his hands to his mouth. "He's probably still in the cabinet. Unless he has found the lever to release the mechanism."

"Go home, right now. Look," she said, "I'll pay for a cab, if you can find one. Wait here." She ran around the side of the house and entered by the scullery door, pushing past Nettie as she hurled herself along the cold corridors at the back, the secret ways used the servants to pass invisibly through the warren of a house. She grabbed the very last of her funds and came back to Simeon, panting and sweating. Her good green dress was not made for exertion.

"Take this, and use it in whatever way you can, to get back to your rooms as quickly as possible. See to Tobias. I hope that he is all right. Stay inside. Don't worry about a thing. I'll sort my father out."

132

"But you don't know where he has gone!"

"He said he was going to use his contacts. Well," she said with a firm air. "I am going to use *mine*."

***

Reassuring Simeon was one thing. She had managed to hide her fear and panic from him, and he seemed a little calmer as he left, rushing off into the night. He was relieved that he had passed on the message, and therefore the responsibility of fixing things was no longer his.

She stood on the stone steps with the noise and the chaos of the house behind her muffled by the door. She was separate from it and that was both a comfort and a terror. There was a gas lamp up high to her right and she didn't want to step out of its pool of light.

But her father was out there, marauding around London, terrifying her friends and possibly ill, as his brain-fevers grew more severe. She ran through her options.

She could go to the theatre that the Clay brothers had been working at, and ask the manager or some staff to give her information. Then what? Go on alone, intercept her father, and bring him home?

It sounded fine in principle. But the night was creeping on. She was a woman of lower-middling standing. She could walk alone, but she would not walk at night without inviting comment and abuse. She had a small pistol but what could that do if she were surrounded by a ring of men? Would she shoot them all?

She could take a hint from popular novels, the sort she devoured from the circulating libraries, where the doughty heroines took up disguises. She had done so herself, for another case. But what disguise could let a woman pass in the rough streets? Only the disguise of a man. And she didn't think she could pull that off convincingly. Men walked differently, talked differently. She could not hope to adjust her gait, used as she was to years of tiny hobbling steps. She could not stride with a masculine confidence. She could try, but she knew she would fail. If it were full winter, she could hide herself in a cloak. In the hinterlands of autumn, that would simply draw attention to her.

She scuffed her foot against the step in frustration. She had to act. But she could not act alone. She half-considered turning back into the house and asking Mr Barrington to accompany her. He was small and round and would possibly be of use if she bowled him at people, like a large ball, to scatter anyone who got in their way.

No. She knew of one person, and one person only, who could possibly have the skills and the willingness to help her in this kind of matter.

She remembered his address. He took rooms in an apparently respectable house, retaining a daily girl and a man servant too, and had worked on private business for Lord Hazelstone, amongst others. He was outwardly a gentleman.

But Jack Monahan was nothing of the sort.

She didn't want to get in touch with him.

Yet he was exactly who she needed now.

Fourteen

Thank goodness there were frequent trains criss-crossing the whole of the South East of England. She was in London within thirty minutes, but she stepped away from the train station and into a different world. It was still London: but at night.

She hailed a cab and directed him to Jack's street. She felt a curious anticipation rise in her throat and her stomach fluttered with nerves. She had vowed never to cross Jack Monahan's path again, and he hadn't seemed too bothered about that. He was a cocky, arrogant, infuriating man. Yet she felt strangely concerned about him, too. Almost maternal, in a way, or fraternal perhaps; he would have made an ideal older brother.

She knocked at the door and the housekeeper answered. She did not recognise Marianne until she spoke.

"Mrs Hathaway? How lovely to see you again. It is Miss Starr. Might Mr Monahan be available?"

"Really? I mean, of course. It's you … I remember you. Won't you step inside? I'll call him." Mrs Hathaway was shaking her head as she turned away, dismissing Marianne as now some tragic fallen woman. She waited in the hallway. A smell of boiled mutton came rolling from a distant room. Mrs Hathaway came back down the stairs.

"He says that you are to go on up. First door that you see. Hmm. We are a respectable house but he assures me you won't be here on anything other than business. Might I suggest, then, that in future you stick to business hours? I do not want the neighbours to talk."

Suitably reprimanded, Marianne went upstairs, feeling more nervous by the minute, but also affronted at Mrs Hathaway's insinuations.

When she reached the landing, Jack Monahan was waiting for her, leaning on the doorframe of his open door. He was dressed for an evening at home, in his shirtsleeves and loose jacket, and didn't have anything on his feet except for holed socks. He grinned in a triumphant way, like he'd won something.

She felt immediately defensive, and vulnerable. Was visiting a man like this, alone in his house, any better than wandering the streets? No. Not really. At least no one knew that she was here. That was actually a positive though it ought not to have been.

Yet for all his louche air, she trusted him.

"Oh, Marianne, what a delight it is to see you again! You should have sent word ahead."

"So that you could put some shoes on?"

"So that I could have had better wine to offer you. Please do step inside."

"This is not a social call."

"It is nearly eight o'clock. If it is business, I can only imagine what business that might be, and you have sadly fallen in the world."

"No, it is not really business, either. I need help."

"You need wine. Here."

She followed him into his room. He thrust a glass at her, and motioned for her to sit down. His room was remarkably comfortable, furnished in strong male shades of brown and deep red. There was a crackling fire in the grate, something that Marianne had missed under the strict reign of Mrs Davenport's economy. She sipped at the wine, trying to absorb its confidence but not the mind-numbing effects, and admired the hunting scenes adorning his walls.

"So, how can I help you?" he asked, and he looked so punchable and smug that for a moment she regretted coming at all.

"You know most people in London," she said. She didn't bother with niceties or anything that would waste time or potentially distract the conversation from its purpose. "I have an issue with my father. He is on the warpath and he is out, on his own somewhere in London, intending to challenge two brothers. They might not be brothers, actually, but they perform illusions as the Marvellous Brothers Clay."

"Go on."

"This is awkward. Forgive me. My friend Simeon – do you remember him?"

"I do. Pale sort of chap. Needs a meal and a night out, if you know what I mean."

"I hope I do *not*. Well, he built a magical cabinet for these men, who took off with the cabinet and his money."

"How on earth does this involve your father?"

"I am not entirely sure," she admitted. "I had loaned some money to Simeon to make this cabinet, and this has left me out of pocket somewhat, due to … other circumstances, which I won't go into. Suffice it to say that I believe my father to have taken up the cudgel, as it were, when he heard of this, and he has gone off to track these men down, in order to obtain the money owing to Simeon – and to me."

"Ahh." Jack nodded, and crossed his legs, letting his foot dangle and bob. He was drinking whisky, not wine, and he drank it slowly, savouring the flavour and aroma. "Well, unfortunately, flattered though I am that you have come to me, I do not know anything about these brothers. I have not heard of them. I do not frequent stage shows, myself. Well, not those kind of shows. Finish your wine; I can take you to my kind of show, if you like."

"I would rather not. It does not matter that you don't know about the brothers. I didn't expect you to. I simply need a man to come with me when I speak to the theatre staff. I have to go now, tonight, to stop my father before he does something that might involve the police. Or worse. First, then, I need to find him, and the theatre manager is the only chance I have."

"You want me to be your chaperone."

"I do. Please."

"No, but thank you for the invitation."

"What can I offer you, that might induce you to help me?"

He laughed. "You can't pay me; you've admitted that."

"How are you working at the moment?" she asked him, bluntly. "You know that I can perhaps influence things, through my sister and her husband; even through my father."

138

He looked at her with condescension. "It is not quite the influence that I need, but thank you all the same. More wine? How is the fog tonight?"

"Thick and cloying, much like you."

"Ouch. All because you have nothing that I need or want. Well…"

"Oh, stop that." But she accepted more wine. He topped up his own glass with whisky while he was at it. When he settled himself back by the fire, she asked, "What do you want, more than anything in the world?"

"There's a question. You first. What do you want?"

"Freedom."

"Pfft. That's a woolly concept. You are free. Do you work in a factory? Are you in a sanatorium? Do you labour in a mine? Have you twenty-seven children and a drunkard for a husband? You *are* free, Marianne."

She took a gulp of wine that was rather too large. "Freedom to live in my own place, with my own money, and freedom from interference from others."

"Oh, *that* kind of life? I have it and I can tell you this: it's lonely. I wouldn't recommend it."

"I need to try it. Maybe it will suit me, maybe it won't. So, I have told you my dream. And yours?"

"I just alluded to it," he said, turning away to gaze into the fire. Maybe her honesty had loosened his tongue – along with the whisky. "This freedom is wearing on me. I want a wife."

She winced. "Look, Jack, I do like you but…"

"Oh, God, not you!" he spluttered, laughing. "Sorry,

Marianne, I was not angling into a proposal in any way. You have made your feelings perfectly plain and anyway, you would make a poor wife. I would know you were chafing, longing for freedom all the time, after all!"

"Oh. Oh, I see. Good."

There followed a supremely awkward silence. Well, Marianne felt uncomfortable, at least. She stole a sidelong glance at Jack and saw that he was staring intently into the fire, his face blank.

She said, carefully, "I could find a suitable wife for you, you know. I've been learning all about this marriage market from my cousin's mother."

He snorted and continued to watch the flames.

"No, I am serious. Please. I'm not mocking you at all, Jack."

The use of his name, so personal, so unbidden, startled him. He turned to her. "She would have to be the right sort of woman."

"You must make me a list of what you prefer. Phoebe knows all the useful women in London. We can do this, you know, if we know your preferences. Short, tall, blonde, dark … whatever. Accomplished, educated – or not."

"Is that what you think men want? She can be red-headed and dance like a rock falling down the stairs for all I care. She must understand me. That's what is important. She must stand by my side and look forward to the same horizon, do you see? We do not need to look at one another. We need to be partners looking to the same future." He slammed back the remains of his drink and leaped to his feet. "Oh, drat and confound you, Marianne. Let me find some suitable shoes."

Fifteen

"This is a shoddy, two-bit, run-down, belly-up kind of a place," Jack said with glee as he helped Marianne down from the cab outside the theatre. He paid the driver and she didn't object. The cab rumbled away. Jack beat his gloved hands together and gazed up at the blackened edifice down the side street of Soho.

"It seems all closed up. I suppose that they mustn't be running a show tonight."

People hurried to and fro, passing the end of the street, dipping in and out of the glow of the street lights and being absorbed into the ubiquitous fog that was crawling its way out of the Thames. The city would be submerged and stifled by the stuff for the next six months, and when it faded away for the summer, it would be replaced by the vile stench of the river cooking in the sun.

Marianne thought that she rather preferred the fog.

She turned her attention back to the gloomy backstreet theatre. "Are we even facing the main doors?" she asked as she examined them. They were large, wooden and had paint peeling from them like strips of flayed flesh, it had been so thickly painted on over the years. Handbills and posters were pasted in a haphazard fashion over every spare inch of wall. The windows were blacked out, and no lamp showed, either outside or within.

"I think so," Jack said. He strode up and thumped hard on the door with his gloved fist.

The door was flung open almost immediately and Jack leaped back. Neither of them had expected such a prompt response. The man who now faced out from the pitch-black interior looked furious. He was of middling height for a man, just an inch or two taller than Marianne herself, and had a strangely doll-like face, smooth and taut. His large eyes were pale blue, and his cheeks were reddened in a way that would make maidens jealous.

"Now what?" he demanded. "Oh – who in the blazes are you?"

He was addressing Jack, but Marianne stepped up and extended her hand. "I am Miss Starr, and this is Mr Monahan. We were wondering if you had seen someone of some importance, well, of importance to us. A Mr Russell Starr? Tall, imposing sort of man…"

"If by imposing you mean he's a raving monster with wild eyes and a tendency to lunge, then yes, I have seen him. Starr, and Starr. Relation, is he? Needs locking up. Threatened me. Threatened me!"

"I am so very sorry to hear that," Marianne said, cringing. "He is my father and he has been under considerable stress lately. He is not himself. I imagine that he was asking for information about the Clay Brothers?"

"The Marvellous Brothers Clay, yes, well, he was, and I told him what I knew, and off he went, but not before breaking a lamp. Your father was he, eh? Well, you can pay for the damage."

Unlikely, Marianne thought, unless he was going to accept payment in buttons or bottles of useless chemicals. "What exactly did you tell him?"

"Going to pay, are you? Good lamp, it was."

Jack stepped up to the top step and loomed over the theatre proprietor. It was a very effective loom, and had the other man pressing his back against the doorjamb. Jack also had a pretty good line in sinister voices. He spoke in a low tone, entirely too reasonably to be trustworthy, and very close to the man's face. Just watching the performance made Marianne shudder as she imagined the hot breath on her own skin.

"I have many ways of *paying*," Jack said. "Would you like a demonstration, or shall we progress immediately to simply meeting this good lady's request? Hmm?"

It was strange how one could imply the breaking of bones in such an innocent-sounding way. The theatre manager gave up immediately. His was a world of fake violence, not the real stuff.

"Canterbury Lane," he squeaked. "Somewhere along there."

Jack was suddenly all joviality. He clapped the man on the shoulder, told him that he was a "good fellow", and pushed him back into his own theatre.

Jack and Marianne hurried back to the more well-lit streets. "Do you know it? Is it far?" she asked.

"It's a nasty little back alley behind the Tottenham Court Road. No, it's not far."

143

She kept pace with him as they pushed through the theatre-loving crowds of Soho. "And how do you know of this nasty little back alley?"

"The usual ways," he said, laughing. "And you cannot complain while you find my knowledge useful. Actually there is a woman there – well, she is old, now. Very old. But she was a friend of my mother, and I call on her from time to time."

"Oh…"

"To take her food, and to see if she has enough coal. There, you see, you did not peg me as a charitable man, did you?"

"I did not. But I wager you only do it because she has some use to you, in some way."

"Yes. She knows people. And she will know these brothers, too, especially if they live on the same street as she does. Let us call in on dear old Judy, and mind you watch your manners. She might not be up to your standard of ladylike, but she deserves respect all the same."

"I would not dream of treating anyone as anything less than my own self."

"Hmm."

They were in the back alley within five minutes, and it stank of rotten food, and the manure of animals. "Can I hear a pig?" she asked.

"Perhaps," Jack said. "We're also near a brothel."

"They have animals?"

"No, of course not! You haven't heard the sounds of many brothels, have you?"

"I have heard *none*."

"And you call yourself educated. Come along. You are going to get your skirts dirty."

She picked her way along the grimy street as best she could, given that she could barely see, and her boots slipped on soft, slimy things. She was glad she could not see.

They entered a narrow house where even the corridors seemed to have people asleep in them, lying on the floor, huddled to one another for warmth. Jack led her to a ground floor room at the back, a tiny cupboard of a place next to the shared scullery, with only enough room for a narrow plank for a bed and a few twigs of furniture.

Judy was ancient, and bundled up in layers of blankets like a swaddled baby. She sat on her bed, and Marianne and Jack stood. She tittered like a little girl, but Marianne heeded Jack's words and spoke to her with careful respect. Jack himself fussed around her, setting things straight on the wobbly table, poking at the tiny makeshift fire, bringing her tea with brandy in it, and finally prising out the information that they had come for.

When they left, Marianne felt she had seen a new side to Jack. She said, as they walked the few yards up the alley, "You know, I really shall find you just the perfect wife."

"Not now, Marianne," he replied testily, and her good feeling almost vanished. "This is the door. Now, do you have any kind of plan, assuming that they are home? What if your father has been and gone?"

She heard shouting, but it did not come from inside the house. She turned and saw a dot of light swinging at waist height, approaching from the far end of Canterbury Lane. It got larger and threw up uncanny shadows on the face of the man carrying it.

"He has not been and gone," she said, wearily. "Here he comes now."

"How did we beat him here?"

She laughed, but felt no humour in it. "I suspect I know the answer. He is not used to travelling in London. He would not have known the way, or at least, he would not remember it from his youth. So he would have hailed a cab. But I wager no cab would drive him. Father!"

"Marianne? What in the devil? Do you know, they said I was drunk! Me! I told him, I said, I am a world-famous chemist. And one man said – well, I shall not repeat what he said. The cove! It would sully your ears."

"Ears can't be sullied. You're a scientist. You know that. And I've heard the sounds of a brothel already tonight, so I'm probably already doomed. I still think it might have been pigs," she added, glancing at Jack. "Anyway, father. You have come here to speak to the Clay Brothers, is that right?"

"It is. Is this the house? Oh – oh! Hello, sir. I remember this cad. Jack. You broke into Price's study!"

"Delighted to make your acquaintance once more," Jack said, extending his hand like they were in a comfortable club.

Russell slapped it away. "I warned you. I can't remember what I warned you, but the warning still stands. I will not hesitate to shoot you. Or worse."

"If I…?"

"If I feel like it. Now, as for these brothers. Are they home?"

146

The three of them regarded the door. Jack started to say, "Well, there is a light up there in the window…"

Marianne sighed, and simply knocked on the door.

"You've blown our secrecy."

"We are standing in the middle of the street and talking loudly. How furtive could we be? Did you have a plan?"

"I was formulating one."

Their bickering was interrupted when the door opened and a young man stood there, his shirt sleeves rolled up. He had an angular face, all planes and edges, and a wisp of a dirty brown beard that failed to cover his pink, blotched skin.

"Mr Clay?" she asked.

"Um. Maybe?"

"Are you one of the famous Marvellous Brothers Clay?"

"Oh, yeah, I am. Um. Jeremiah's in the back."

Jack laughed. "You're not brothers, are you?"

"Nah, but it sounds good."

"Are you even called Clay?"

"Yeah, I am. I'm Tom Clay. He ain't." Tom twisted his head around and yelled, "Je-ere-miah!"

Russell moved without warning, taking the chance to leap forward and grab Tom around the neck while his attention was elsewhere.

Tom, in spite of his underfed frailty, slammed Russell against the wall, trapping his fingers, making Russell yelp and let go with one hand. It was enough for Tom to be able to shake free and he ran along the dark and dingy corridor towards the back of the house, yelling, "Jerry, arm yourself! We are under attack!"

"Damn." Jack launched himself after them, closely followed by Marianne and Russell who was muttering curses under his breath.

They cornered Tom in the kitchen at the back of the house. It was a steamy, foetid room, with damp washing hanging on a wooden frame from the ceiling, and a smell of over-boiled potatoes in the air. Tom had grabbed hold of a long-handled metal ladle, and was brandishing it with a still and steady hand. That was far more terrifying than any flamboyant waving. "Who are you? What do you want?"

The other man, that they supposed to be Jeremiah, was holding a carving knife. He was taller than Tom, with the same slenderness except for a pot belly and fat, bulging eyes with a thick neck that looked strange on his wiry frame.

Russell noticed him and pointed a finger. "Iodine," he said. "I wager that you feel cold all the time, don't you?"

"Huh?"

"You need to eat seaweed or you'll die."

"Are you threatening me?"

"Not yet. That was just friendly advice. Where's the cabinet?"

Jeremiah and Tom looked at one another. "The cabinet? What are you talking about? We don't even know who you are."

"Come on, stupid boys. I am Russell Starr."

That brought no reaction but confusion.

Russell sighed. "Imbeciles. You bought a magic cabinet from Simeon Stainwright, and then omitted to pay him. So we're here on his behalf to obtain the payment."

"Oh, so you're a bailiff?"

"I am a chemist."

"What?" Tom shook his head. "Well. It's broken anyway."

"What have you done?"

"For God's sake." Tom threw the ladle down on the table. "Look, the cabinet's knackered, all right? It never worked from the start. Honestly, I reckon we ought to ask for our money back."

"You can't ask for your money back when you haven't paid him in the first place!" Marianne spat out.

"Yeah but it's the principle of the thing, ain't it? Are you a lady bailiff? That don't seem right. Not quite natural. But anyway, it were broken so we don't owe nobody nothing."

Her head whirled with the nonsense of it. They seemed to believe that they were in the right. "Where's the cabinet now?" she asked.

"Parlour. We ain't even got it to the theatre. Would have left it there if we had. Useless piece of junk, taking up space."

"Well, we'll take that back with us, too," Russell said.

"You can't. It's ours."

"Oh, this is ridiculous and you are wasting my time," Jack said, interrupting the farcical conversation. He picked up the ladle that Tom had put down, and smacked it hard on Jeremiah's knuckles, causing him to drop the knife. "How much were you supposed to pay for this thing?"

"Three pounds," Jeremiah said, sucking at his bruised hand and scowling.

Marianne winced. That was a lot of money, almost three

guineas. She knew that Simeon's rent was only five shillings a week. Three pounds would keep Simeon in food and materials for a while, even after he had paid her back.

Such blatant robbery seemed to rile Russell and Jack even more, too.

Jack took up the knife. Now he was armed in each hand, if you counted the ladle, and he waved them both vaguely in the air. "Very well, then. Let's have the money, lads."

"No, you can't just…"

Jack thrust the knife at Jeremiah. He jumped back with a squeak. "I can. I'd rather take payment in cash than, I don't know, ears."

"Ears?"

"You heard me. So get us the money *while you still have ears to hear me ask for it.*"

"Jerry, don't do it."

"I'll wave the knife at you, too, and that should change your tune." Jack did exactly as he promised, and Tom too pressed back in horror.

"Yeah, well, all right. But this ain't right. Jerry? Go on, then."

The money turned out to be hidden in an envelope under a metal canister of flour. It was passed to Marianne who counted it, and tucked it away in her handbag. "Thank you," she said. "We are done."

"We're not. If this thing is broken, we'll take it off their hands too," Russell said.

"What?" Jeremiah and Tom chorused.

"Yes, what?" Jack added, equally bemused. "I thought you

were joking."

"I last made a joke in 1867 and no one at the Royal Institution laughed so I vowed to make no more."

Russell left the kitchen and Marianne hurried after him, clutching her bag firmly to her chest. She heard scuffling behind as she left, but she didn't even bother to look around. Jack could handle Tom and Jeremiah.

The parlour was the room at the front of the house, but there was no feminine touch here. It was not a room kept for best, with layers of lace and embroidery, and fancy decorations. Instead it was being used as a general store room with lumber everywhere, and in the middle she spotted the long wooden box that Simeon had made.

"This is it." She went over to it and opened the lid. The mechanism slid smoothly back but something jarred at the very apex of the movement. She wiggled it, but the brothers were correct; perhaps there had been damage caused in transit. No matter, she thought, and closed the lid.

Russell picked up one end. "It is light," he commented. "You can manage this."

"I am a lady, father," she complained, dutifully, but she pushed her bag's handles over her forearm and took hold of the other end of the box.

"I did not raise you to be a lady," he said. He began to walk backwards, unsteadily. "I raised you to be a useful human being."

"Did you imagine we would be roaming the streets of London at night, together, threatening stage magicians?"

He smiled. "I did not. I wish you had met my own mother,

Marianne. This would have amused your grandmother mightily. She was quite remarkable, you know; she had the ear of the Prince Regent, it was said. When I was a young man, she would take me and my brothers travelling all across Europe. She had no time for being told what she could and could not do."

He huffed as he shuffled backwards, and they angled the box to get it out into the hallway. "She always sounded most amazing," Marianne said. "Would I ... do I live up to her expectations?"

"She would be proud of you. So very proud. But as I grew up, the world seemed to change. Society closed in around her. The new Queen brought a new way of life with each child that she had. My father was embarrassed at my mother's independence. He stopped her doing the things that she loved. He had to, you know. To keep his place in society." Russell shook his head. "Society can go to hell. None of it is worth a fig. Steady now! Here comes that ruffian."

She turned and saw that he meant Jack, who was coming down the corridor backwards, his arms out to keep Jeremiah and Tom away from him.

"Go on," Jack yelled over his shoulder at them. "Get out of here!"

"Us?" Marianne said, just as her father started moving again. He wedged the box half against the wall, balancing it on his upraised knee and pulled the street door open.

"Go!" Jack yelled.

Russell blundered out into the street and Marianne rushed after him, trying to keep her grip on the box. Jack came a moment later, still stabbing randomly with the knife and the ladle. Jeremiah and Tom were shouting and throwing things, and the air was thick with cursing and swearing. People poked their heads out of doors and windows, and started to shout and laugh.

The audience worked in their favour. Jeremiah and Tom stopped at their doorway, and Jack ran over to take Marianne's place.

"I am fine. I can manage," she told him.

"Yes, but…"

"And it would mean leaving me in charge of the knife. Which I will willingly brandish," she added. "But you might not like it."

"Damn it." Jack tucked the purloined kitchen knife in his suit pocket and wrestled the box away from Marianne. "There. Lead on."

This time, Russell was able to walk forwards as Jack took the lead in going the wrong way, and Marianne steered them down the alleyway and to the main street. Jeremiah and Tom stayed behind, defeated. They knew they could not take on all three of them, and neither of the showmen were fighters – unlike Jack.

No cab was willing to take them, however. "A coffin? Not likely!" was the general comment, along with jokes and jibes – "Who's dead, then?" and "Vampires, are you?"

So they made slow progress through the streets. The box was not heavy but one person had always to be going backwards. The darkness hid trips and holes, and Marianne took her father's place when they were halfway to Simeon's. They walked in silence now. She kept a careful eye on her father. It was late, and he was not well. She imagined that he had been fuelled, thus far, by rage and drugs, but those things would soon be wearing off.

He knew that she was looking at him. He bristled, and turned his face away.

Sixteen

Simeon was ecstatic for around three whole minutes when they arrived with the cabinet and his money. He directed them to place the box on a set of trestles, and he immediately began to open and close it, trying to find the source of the problem. Russell sank into a chair, and Jack prowled around, poking at things, until a fake rabbit closed its teeth onto his fingers with a mechanical snap, and he yelped and drew away. He pulled the stolen knife from his pocket and said, "So, Simeon, do you need a knife?"

"Um, thanks, why not," Simeon replied. "Can you put it on that table near the kettle?"

"Other people ask where the knife has come from," Marianne pointed out.

"Well, I assume it's from a kitchen or a shop. Oh, look, the problem is with the runner here, do you see? It has warped. The wood was not dry enough. What a bother. I shall have to undo this whole side of the box…"

Marianne took what was owing to her from the envelope and lodged the rest on the table, next to the knife. She said, "You ought to be careful who you do business with."

"I don't have a great deal of choice. You *told* me to make things for others."

"This whole affair is hardly my fault."

"All's well that ends well," Jack said, suddenly the peacemaker.

Simeon stopped and stood straight up, wild-eyed and fearful. "They know where I live! They will come back for the money! They will!"

"They will not. Anyway, you are not alone here any longer. Where is Tobias?" Marianne asked. "Dear God, please tell me that you've released him from wherever he was trapped."

"He is hiding."

"From us?"

"Yes. I told him to."

"But why?"

"Just in case. After all, your father did menace me."

"Oh, Simeon. You are *infuriating*." She looked around the chaotic workshop and called, in a loud voice, "Tobias, ignore what this buffoon tells you. You can come out. Anyway, I need to ask you something."

The boy sidled out from behind a mirror. He looked at Jack and Russell in alarm, and didn't say anything.

"Come, come. Sit with me. Um, Simeon, is this couch safe to sit on?" She indicated a long sofa with floral patterns of pink and red.

"Yes, but don't press the panel on the end," he said.

She took a seat, and gingerly patted the cushion next to her.

Tobias came over reluctantly and sat with his hands clamped on his knees, his legs together, and his shoulders hunched over.

"Tobias, who do you think killed your great aunt?"

"I don't know."

"I know that it wasn't you," Marianne said, trying to sound confident. Did she know? Did she really? "I suspect that it was someone else in the household. What do you think?"

"I don't know."

"Mrs Peck had no reason to do it, of course."

"No, she wouldn't."

"But what of your aunt, Mrs Newman?"

"I don't know."

"Do you get on with her? Do you like her?"

"She's loud. She tries to be kind, in her way. I don't know."

Russell had been listening to his daughter's painful attempts to establish a rapport with the young man. He grabbed a wooden chair and sat down opposite them. He leaned forward.

"You, there. Now listen. Someone did for the old lady and we need to find out who that was."

Tobias couldn't bring himself to utter "I don't know" again. He froze and stared at Russell.

Marianne said, "Tell us absolutely everything about Mrs Newman."

"Um. She came back from America. Her husband's dead. She came to Rosedene."

"Was Miss Dorothea happy to see her?"

"No. But Mrs Newman wasn't happy to see my great aunt, either. I think she thought she had already died."

"Why would she be disappointed that she was still alive? Oh yes. I think that Mrs Newman expected to inherit Rosedene."

Tobias shook his head. "I don't think she cares about Rosedene. She kept telling my aunt that she should sell it and move away."

"Well, she wanted the money then." It was the most obvious, simple and understandable motivation for many things – including murder.

"Maybe. I don't know."

Marianne felt like she was banging her head against a brick wall. "What else can you tell us about her?"

"Nothing."

"Where did she go? Who did she see? Did she receive callers?"

"No. She went into London but I don't think she saw anyone. She would come home annoyed. She was always annoyed. I stayed out of her way."

"What about your great aunt?"

"Aunt Dorothea didn't like her at all. I don't know why. She said she should have stayed in America."

"Did you know you were the sole beneficiary in the will?"

"No, but I did wonder when that man came to do it."

Marianne closed her eyes and inhaled. She opened them to see Russell, Jack and Simeon all watching and listening closely, all of a sudden.

"Go on. What man?"

"The man that came to do the will."

"When?"

"After the other man."

Marianne had to sit on her hands to prevent herself from leaping up and strangling the boy. She waited for him to elaborate. As the silence lengthened, Tobias realised he was supposed to tell them more.

"So, well, first this one man came, and he was from an auction house, and my great-aunt Dorothea said for Mrs Newman not to know about it, but she was out in town so it didn't matter, and I showed him up to my great-aunt and they talked for a while and then he went away."

"Which auction house?"

"I don't know. They had a silly name. It was long and repeated itself and sounded like Latin so I didn't listen because I don't like Latin. Except I do. I miss it now I am not at school. I want to go and learn Latin again."

Russell said, "That will be Atticus, Purfoy and Atticus."

"That is it. So he came and went. And then Great Aunt Dorothea asked me to bring Mr Unthank, that solicitor man, to her, so I did."

"Ahh. Was she rewriting her will?"

"That's what I thought, and I don't know if it's a sin or not but I did wonder who was going to get her house and her money. I didn't know it was going to be me, though. I didn't know. I promise. I swear it…" He bent his head and a tear dropped onto his trousers.

"I know, I know," Marianne said.

"Pfft," said Jack, and to Marianne's surprise, he was hushed by her father.

Marianne patted Tobias's hand. He flinched but remained as still as he could. "It is late," she said. "We should go. But I promise you that we will avenge your great aunt. Oh, one last thing. Do you have any idea where Mrs Newman might have gone?"

"America?" the boy said.

"I hope not," Marianne replied with gritted teeth. "Come on, father. It is time to get you to bed."

"I rather hoped Jack might take us to a party. It looks like the sort of thing he would do."

"Oh, you're best of friends now, are you?"

Jack grinned at her in triumph while Russell blinked in confusion. "Actually, I am rather tired…"

Jack caught his arm as the older man stumbled. She bid Simeon good night, although he looked as if he were going to work into the small hours, and followed the two men out into the night. At this late time of night, it would be at least another hour before they were all safely tucked up in bed.

***

Marianne curled in her bed, and pulled the covers up over her face to block the light that Phoebe had so rudely let flow into her bedroom.

"Close them," she growled from the depths of her warm nest.

"I've brought you toast and eggs. Mrs Cogwell has done that sauce you like. She must be stockpiling and hiding food.

Good on her. And there is coffee, and tea too. But you must sit up and tell me everything. Marianne! Why are you still dressed?"

"Half dressed," Marianne said, as she clawed her way up to lean back on the pillows. "I did take out anything that might puncture a lung in the night." She still wore her softer undergarments, her skirts and her jacket. It would be creased and possibly ruined. "I was so very cold."

"Barrington says you did not come in until three in the morning."

"That sounds likely. I don't recall the exact time."

"And Jack Monahan was with you!"

"He insisted on seeing us home but he did not stay. He went off to do whatever it is men like him do at night." She remembered the alleyway. "It might involve pigs."

"How dreadful," Phoebe said in delight and sat on the side of the bed. "You must tell me everything!"

"Eggs, you say?"

"Here." Phoebe pointed at the tray resting on the end of the bed. She passed it over. In payment, Marianne told her cousin everything.

"I am so glad you got your money back, too!" Phoebe said. "I was wondering if…"

"No. I simply cannot advance any more loans."

"I thought not." She sighed. "Well, we must press on though we walk through a valley of tears, or something like that. My mother's daily prayers are such a bind. And what is your plan for the rest of the day?"

"How much of it is left?"

"If you rise now, you will have at least the afternoon."

"Good. I need to pay a call on Atticus, Purfoy and Atticus."

"Who are they? Can I come with you?"

"Will your mother allow it?"

Phoebe pouted. "It is like I am twelve years old again. I simply shan't tell her, Marianne. I will dress down and come with you in secret. And you will need to avoid my mother, anyway. She is *furious* about your antics."

Marianne thought about it. "Very well. Come with me; I should enjoy the company. But don't dress down. This is a fine auction house we are visiting. In fact – will you dress up?"

Seventeen

Atticus, Purfoy and Atticus were not quite in the same league of the large, famous auction houses such as Christie and Manson's or the like, but they rubbed shoulders close enough to St James's as to make no difference, Albemarle Street being respectable enough and within sight of the hallowed district. Phoebe looked entirely at ease as she picked her way delicately along the crowded pavement. Marianne had done her best with her own appearance, and probably passed as the poor relation – which she was. They had also brought Mr Fry, Price's valet, to follow behind, ready to carry parcels, open doors, fend off footpads and generally look the part.

"Your mother should be proud of you," Marianne said, remembering her out-of-character conversation with her own father the previous night. Clearly his sudden attack of sympathetic emotion had been brought on by stress. "You are every inch the well-bred lady."

"That is down to my schooling, I think, and my natural inclinations. You remember how mother was, when we were children."

"I confess I hardly remember a thing. She was just a blur in the background."

"That is true. I had intended to be so very different with Gertie and Charlie ... but oh, they are taking so long to get interesting!"

"You do your part. You read to them, don't you?" Admittedly, Marianne thought, Phoebe was trying to get her eight year old daughter interested in *Clarissa*, unsuccessfully, but it was something. Just the close proximity of mother and daughter was important, wasn't it?

"I try. I am supposed to guide them in their moral education. Really, I simply want them to be happy. And rich. I suppose those are the same things."

"Perhaps. Ah – this is it."

The front of the premises was narrow and the main door was locked. Mr Fry rang the bell and they were let in by a uniformed doorman. They passed through the large doors. Security was paramount in such a business; even the windows had curious collections of wires and metal on them, which would sound alarms if tampered with, an American invention which interested Marianne deeply. The doorman took them past desks and clerks and into a long, high-ceilinged hall at the back of the premises. There were no sales scheduled for that day, but still the place teemed with prospective buyers examining the lots, clutching catalogues, and conferring with their confederates in low and learned tones. Everyone wanted to sound as if they knew exactly what they were talking about.

The doorman brought them to a closed-off room at the

back, and knocked, and after a quick discussion, they were ushered into the presence of Mr Atticus himself, though whether it was the first or the last in the name of the company, Marianne had no idea. Mr Fry remained outside the door, close enough at hand to burst to their aid if they shouted.

Mr Atticus was young, black-haired, and stout, with a yellowish tint to his eyes and skin as white and pale as a fine bone-china cup. He bounced to his feet and shook their hands with great enthusiasm.

He got down to business straight away. "Lovely to meet you, lovely, lovely. I am in rather in a rush – you can make an appointment if you prefer – but I do have a spare moment, so, dear ladies, how may I help you?" He might have been overwhelmed with work, but he clearly didn't want to miss an opportunity for potential business.

Phoebe looked to Marianne. She leaned forward. "I am assisting Inspector Gladstone of Scotland Yard in a murder enquiry."

"You are a lady. I find it unlikely. Dashed exciting! But unlikely." He smiled to soften the blow of his suspicion.

"Well, you may send word to him to ask. Let me tell you who has been killed, and then you may reconsider the unlikeliness of what I say. Do you recollect going to see an elderly woman, Miss Dorothea Newman, who was confined to her bed in a house called Rosedene? If it were not you, it was one of your partners here."

"Miss Dorothea Newman! I do not forget her. Indeed, it was I who went. And how do you know about this?"

"I told you the truth. I am aiding the police. I was initially called in to investigate the paranormal activity – supposed paranormal activity – occurring in the building. Here is my card." Marianne slipped a firm and elegant rectangle over to the auctioneer.

"Miss Starr. Well, well. So you are turned detective now? I should ask, is it Miss Newman who has been killed?"

"The very same."

"Sad. Dashed sad news. She was a rare one. And murder, you say?"

"Undoubtedly. And not long after your visit to her. That brings us to our purpose. I must ask you, what did she want to see you about?"

Mr Atticus took a moment to gather his thoughts. She could see that underneath his bubbling energy, there was a keen mind and a precise judge of events. "Ordinarily we do not disclose private transactions. Yes, much of what we do is open and public, but sometimes people approach us to dispose of valuable items in confidence, and that was the case in this instance. However, as the main party is now deceased, God rest her soul, I feel able to speak. Miss Newman had requested that some jewellery be sold on her behalf."

"Were they particularly valuable pieces?"

"Very much so. There is a necklace in gold set with a range of precious stones. Rather gaudy for today's taste, but of considerable value nonetheless. It is part of a set, including a pair of earrings, and some bracelets, and a matching brooch with an emerald of unusual size, and a notebook detailing the entire provenance of the jewellery."

"Goodness me. And have you been able to sell these items?"

"We have had a number of expressions of interest but the final sale has not yet taken place. We are – and remain to be – keen to secure the very best price for Miss Newman, or in this case, for her descendants. The monies will now go to whoever is named in her will." He looked concerned. "I do hope she has made adequate legal provision, or it leads us to something of a problem."

"Indeed," Marianne said. "I can assure you that those matters are in hand. As for the potential purchasers, are any of them particularly known to Miss Newman? Have you noticed any connections?" Anyone called Mrs Newman, she thought. Although she would hardly use her own name, would she?

"No. They are all unconnected collectors of such things. I do not think that this will go to a public auction. We have a certain list of buyers who are keen to see items like this when they appear; many of the most priceless artefacts never go to public auction at all."

"I see. Please do keep us informed of the progress of the sale. As for the legal matters, those are being dealt with by Mr Unthank. Thank you so much for your time."

***

Marianne's mind was a whirl of questions and she stayed quiet as they walked along Pall Mall. Phoebe was drinking in the atmosphere, though she had no money at all to spend. Mr Fry followed at a suitable distance.

Did Louisa Newman know about the jewels' existence, and had she discovered Miss Dorothea's plans for them to be sold? That was Marianne's main question. Did she think that those jewels ought to have been hers? Why had she first gone to America with her husband? What had happened to him out there?

She absolutely had to find Mrs Newman. She hoped that Tobias was wrong, and that she had not fled back to America. How could she, anyway? She had no money. Who else could know where she had gone? Then the answer came to her: the invisible overlooked class of servants, of course. Mrs Peck, the housekeeper. She would know a lot.

She might know everything.

"I need to go back to Rosedene," Marianne told Phoebe.

"What for?"

"I need to speak to Mrs Peck and the other servant at the house. She was a daily girl who came in when needed, so I think she must live close by, and hopefully I can find out from neighbours where Mrs Peck might be."

"I am tired."

"Go home. Mr Fry will take you. I'll go part of the way by train but then there is more walking."

"Ugh, walking. I will abandon you, if you don't mind?"

"Of course I don't mind. You have other issues, anyway. How are you going to get your mother to leave?"

"Oh, don't," Phoebe said with an exaggerated shudder. "Poison her or marry someone – the choice is yours. I'm afraid it's all down to you, Marianne. Please hurry."

"Hmm." She pressed her lips tightly together and did not trust herself to give an answer to that.

168

Marianne turned herself into a pure detective. She went around the back of the next house along the road nearest to Rosedene and found a scullery maid happy to talk to her. The girl had heard of the "ghosts" but she was a sensible sort of person, and dismissed them as "nonsense". She was a religious type and told Marianne, very confidently, that the only ghost was the Holy Ghost and anything else was "man-made silliness."

"Excellent. What do you know of Mrs Newman?"

"Mrs – oh, the younger woman, the American lady? Nothing at all. Hardly saw her."

"And the older, Miss Dorothea Newman?"

"Lovely woman, everyone said, but I never met her. May she rest in peace."

"Did you know the staff there?"

"Yes. Mrs Peck was friendly enough. Letitia didn't ever say much."

"She was the daily girl?"

"Yes. She's gone away now to some farm in Surrey and maybe that will suit her better."

"And Mrs Peck?"

"She's inside. She's come to work here."

"Ah!"

But what seemed like a stroke of luck turned sour almost immediately. Mrs Peck could offer no solution as to where Mrs Newman had gone, nor did she know anything about any jewellery, or so she said. She spoke curtly and unwillingly and soon went back to her duties.

Marianne found herself standing outside Rosedene, on the gravel, looking up at the strange house, so stubbornly silent and full of secrets.

Everything leaves a trace, Marianne thought. Nothing that has happened in that place can be invisible to science.

What could have caused the screaming? And then she thought – hold hard, there is another question to ask.

Is the screaming sound still occurring at night? Mrs Newman said it had stopped. But I do not trust a word that she says.

For if it was still happening, even intermittently, that would answer so many questions.

She wondered if it were connected to a clock. But they had said it happened on an irregular basis. A broken clock, perhaps? It sounded like speech, but imperfectly so. And if it did occur, it would occur only once a night, and not be repeated. Something on a rough twenty-four hour schedule then, that sometimes worked and sometimes did not. What could that be?

She stared at the windows, willing them to reveal something to her, and then laughed at herself for her own wishful thinking. She'd be attending séances as a participant at this rate. No, Marianne, she reprimanded herself. Let there be science, and only that.

She wandered around the house again, following the same route that she had before. What could *sound* like a voice, screaming? A squeaking door, a hinge that needed oiling. A loose catch banging in the wind. She had walked past inn signs that sounded like the hounds of hell in a stiff breeze. The wind, blowing down a narrow pipe, when it was just in the right direction.

A hidden phonograph – but she had checked every part of the house and so had the police.

She came to the door that she had failed to pick, and tried the handle again, but of course it did not shift. She kicked at the stone step and continued on, looking for anything she might have missed. She'd crawl in through a window if she were able to.

The back of the house was not neat and flat. There were alcoves and jutting rooms, with small windows and large ones, wooden hatches and shutters, and openings with bars across them. It was the best way to make use of space, and ensure that storerooms and larders had ventilation and access. In one corner she came across another door, and as soon as she saw it, she knew that was her way in. She had thought it was an outside store before, but it could also lead inside.

This door was small and wooden, and the marks on the moss on the flagstones showed that it only ever opened halfway, and then rarely. She pulled at it and it scraped unwillingly open. She ducked into a tiny, dark, incredibly chilly little room with no natural light, and stone shelves that were apparently empty.

It didn't matter what it had housed. She found another door and this was locked, but the key remained in the hole and it was not turned. She pushed her handkerchief under the gap at the bottom of the door, using a stick that she found outside. Then she used the same stick to poke the key through the lock until it fell to the floor, and she could pull her handkerchief back with the key now resting on it. It was no work at all to unlock the door and gain access to the main part of the house.

She quashed the little voice in her head that was telling her this was all hopeless. She walked as quietly as she could along the corridor. The floor was made of red quarry tiles and her outdoor boots clicked, echoing off the white-painted walls. She found the kitchen and looked around. It was as Mrs Peck had left it when she had gone, albeit that she had not gone far. A few drawers in the long dresser were half-open. The large table was strewn with items – a colander, a box that had contained tea, a milk jug of stale and rancid cheese-like stuff now.

Somewhere, possibly upstairs, something rattled. Marianne held her breath.

Oh, it was nothing, she told herself. Remember that this house has rats. There could be birds trapped here. Or a loose casement.

Nevertheless, she proceeded with even more caution as she made her way into the Tudor-style hall. The windows here had been boarded up from the outside, and only a small amount of light filtered in from gaps at the top. It was gloomy, and if she had been prone to fancies, she would have fled by now.

The stairs were carpeted and she was able to creep to the next floor in silence. Once again she was drawn to the wing of the house that had been inhabited. She spent fifteen minutes in the Grand Bedroom, gazing around, trying to see what she had missed.

Nothing.

What of the unused parts of the house? She made her way across the landing and explored the other wing. It was as she had expected — bare, empty rooms that smelled of mould and desolation. The floors were thick with dust and mildew clogged the drapery. Wallpaper peeled from the walls and lumps of plaster had fallen down in places. She trudged back to the central landing again, and stood in thought.

A scraping noise at the front door paralysed her.

Someone was unlocking it and they were coming in.

She remained where she was, hidden in the gloom, waiting to see who it was. She pressed a hand to her belly in relief when she recognised the familiar dark uniform of a police constable.

"Good day, sir," she said as she began to walk down the stairs.

He screamed, then got control of himself and turned the scream into a low cough. "Miss. Miss Starr! Ah, was it you all along?"

"I have been here around an hour. How long is *all along*?"

"Not long enough. I have been sent on account of reports of noise and lights here."

"From the neighbours?"

"From the house over the road, opposite; their upper rooms have some view of part of this house. Otherwise, it is quite well screened. But also a passing tradesman noticed a light go out, when he was on an early morning round, and he had called here on the off chance that someone still lived here. That was before we boarded up the windows. He thought nothing of the light until talking to his friends, a few days later, when they told him that the house was empty and the old lady had died, and so he came to us to report it."

"Did Inspector Gladstone send you?"

"Indeed he did, miss. So if the light was not caused by you, then who?"

Marianne now had a pretty good idea of who. "Someone is still living here."

"Where? Have you evidence?"

"Infuriatingly, no. I have searched everywhere."

"Forgive me, miss, but I will conduct a search of my own."

"Indeed, you must, for you may spot what I have missed."

She could not remain in the dark hall. She went outside and stood in the porch, where it was slightly warmer than inside, even in spite of the lack of sunshine. She waited until the constable had finished his search, and when he came out defeated, she accompanied him back to the police station.

She found Inspector Gladstone with a plate of sandwiches on one side of his desk, and a stack of papers on the other. He seemed up to his elbows in both matters. He waved her into a seat opposite his desk, and the constable brought her a fresh cup of tea.

"What of these noises and lights at Rosedene?" she asked immediately. "You sent that man to investigate."

He tapped his pencil on a piece of paper and shook his head. "Oh, I think there is nothing in it, but the neighbours expected a response. There were rats there – you said so yourself."

"Rats cannot light a gas lamp."

"But the moon can shine into a room and reflect off a mirror, when the light is strong enough."

"True, but unlikely. You must think there is *something* to it, to send a constable to investigate."

"As I said, I was merely going through the motions. The house is to be sold, apparently, and I am concerned to keep criminals out. And as you can see, I am rather busy."

It was a hint that she chose to ignore. "Do you know about the jewels?"

"What jewels?"

She told him of her visit to the auction house, and she also explained her theory. "I think the jewels had been hidden somewhere. I do not know if Miss Newman knew about them all along, or discovered them, but she had ordered them to be sold and she changed her will soon afterwards, so that Tobias would inherit everything. And I do not know how much of all that which Mrs Newman knew about, but there is her motive!"

"You truly believe Mrs Newman killed the older Miss Newman?"

"I do."

"In revenge for selling the jewels?"

"Perhaps," she said thoughtfully. "I am not entirely sure why. If she did not know the jewels had been already gone to the auction house, she might have been hastening her inheritance only. That would account for her reaction at the reading of the will."

"But now Mrs Newman is fled."

"No," Marianne said. "I am convinced that she is hiding somewhere in Rosedene."

"We have torn that place apart. You yourself have searched everywhere. It is not possible."

"It must be."

"The theory of the jewels does not hold up. If she thinks they are due to her, why does she not go to the auction house?"

"Perhaps she has no claim. Perhaps she needs some evidence that remains in the house."

"Perhaps she does not know about them at all." Inspector Gladstone laid down his pencil and knitted his fingers together. He looked at her with an expression of benevolent frustration, like a father who was losing patience with a favourite child. "My superiors need a conclusion to this, and Tobias, sadly, looks guilty. More importantly, we know where he is. Yes, I know; he is staying with your odd little friend. He has inherited money; Mrs Newman has not. She gained nothing by the death. By all logic and reasoning, the boy must be the perpetrator."

"Then why have you not arrested him already?" Marianne snapped. "I am sorry – forgive my manner. I am tired."

"No, no. I understand," he replied, looking equally weary. "I should have arrested him a day or so ago. They are snapping at my heels to end this case. I am holding them off, in the hope that you can come up with something, but I cannot hold them off much longer. If you can find Mrs Newman, then I would be willing to interview her again – as forcefully as possible. If you really think she is hiding at Rosedene, I will have the constable give you the key. Go and do what you can."

"Thank you. I cannot ask for more."

"True. You cannot. But you can take a sandwich, if you like."

Eighteen

She did accept a sandwich which was filled with some unidentifiable variant of potted meat, and took the train home, her head filled with possibilities, suspicions, and suppositions. But she was tired, dog-tired in limb and mind, and her thoughts were getting woollier by the minute. She collapsed into bed as soon as she reached her room, and whiled away the evening floating in and out of slumber.

The next day she found she could not avoid taking part in the family prayer session instigated by Ann Davenport. She could feel Mrs Davenport's eyes boring into her as they knelt in the dining room. Prayers were all fine and dandy, Marianne thought, but kneeling as well was going too far. Mrs Davenport had chosen the dining room as being the most appropriate, saying they were to feed on the word of God and receive spiritual sustenance. It impacted on the work of the servants preparing the room for breakfast, but that was of no importance to Mrs Davenport, who insisted that the staff join them if possible, too.

Breakfast, finally, was taken in silence. This suited Price, who always liked to flick through his newspapers, and Marianne was equally relieved. She tried to slip away at the earliest opportunity but Mrs Davenport had been watching her continually, and stopped her with a fierce command.

"Marianne. You and I shall have a private conversation in the library. Come along."

"Mother ..." Phoebe tried to interrupt her.

"Thank you, Phoebe. We will speak later." Mrs Davenport dismissed her daughter as casually as if she were letting a servant return to the kitchen.

Marianne trudged after Mrs Davenport. Phoebe pressed her hand to her eyes and muttered something about a pain in her head.

Marianne was not even allowed to sit down before Mrs Davenport began her assault.

"I am aware that I have little to no jurisdiction or influence over you, Marianne. And this pains me. You are, tragically, an unmarried woman and still therefore under the care of your father. However, we both know that he is often incapable of performing his duties and therefore it apparently falls to me to do my Christian duty in this regard, however unpleasant that might be for the both of us. I take no pleasure in this, Marianne. But I have known you since you were a child. And I fancy that we still might yet have *some* remaining affection for one another."

"Mrs Davenport," Marianne said, choosing her words very carefully. "I am grateful that you care for me. Truly, I am. However, I have lived an independent life for many years now, and –"

"No, you haven't," Mrs Davenport said. "You are not

remotely independent. You live here on my daughter's charity."

"I mean, in matters of morals and ethics and personal choices…"

"Again, I must correct you. You are dependent on Phoebe and Price's largesse. This puts you under an obligation to them. An obligation to not bring shame and dishonour right to their very door."

So they were coming to the crux of the matter. Marianne hung her head. "I am genuinely very, very sorry for any distress my behaviour caused at the dinner party that you had arranged. However, I am really not in the marriage market and…"

"Not only that, but you are running in and out of London, without a single care for your role in the household here, leaving poor Phoebe to cope alone when, if you really embraced your apparent status as a spinster, you should be devoting your life to the ease of others."

"I have not said that I will never marry but not yet, as…"

Mrs Davenport was not going to let her finish a single sentence. The conversation teetered just on the respectable side of what would otherwise be considered an argument as Marianne was informed of her failings, her lack of self-awareness, her pitiful adherence to social convention, her shocking morals and her inevitable decline into solitude, sickness and death. She bit her tongue and remained almost mute, muttering out, "Yes, Mrs Davenport" and "No, Mrs Davenport" at the appropriate points.

By the time she could escape to her room, she was ready to punch a wall, cry a flood of tears, burn the house down, and quite possibly run away to join the circus.

She did none of those things. She sat at her desk, her hands flat on the wooden top, and breathed deeply. She was a mess of emotions on the inside, but she would rather let them consume her from within than let Mrs Davenport know how deeply she had been upset.

There was a restrained tap at her door. Marianne composed herself and invited them in with a word. Emilia de Souza, Phoebe's lady's maid, slipped in and came to Marianne's side.

In a sense, they were roughly equals. Emilia's family was old, and well-respected, and various off-shoots sat in Parliament or held good livings or were high in the military. But Emilia's immediate family had lost their income and so they lived a quieter life, "according to their means." Ann Davenport thought them a very fine example of how people should be, Emilia's "fancy" name notwithstanding.

"God has commanded, and they have obeyed," she had said of the de Souzas.

Marianne took Emilia's hands. The younger woman looked upset, and that was unusual. She usually retained a calm air, even when chaos reigned around. "What's happened?"

"Mrs Cogwell is packing to leave."

"Mrs Cogwell! I know she said that she would but I thought it only an idle threat, and her place here is secure. The male servants are at risk of losing their jobs, yes. And the lower girls. But Mrs Cogwell? We cannot do without a cook!"

"She says she is under too much unnatural pressure, and things have changed, and she is not respected any longer, and she cannot be in a place where she is not trusted. She is seeking a new situation and has already made contact with some agencies."

"Oh …"

"You may swear in front of me."

"I cannot think of words strong enough."

They half-smiled at one another. "Emilia, I don't think there is anything I can do."

But they both knew that there was.

***

She went to see Simeon and Tobias, and wondered whether to ask Simeon if she could move into his workshop with him. Her father could sleep on a truckle bed perhaps.

Then their downfall would be complete. They could not rise up from such a move. It would not be a temporary thing. It would mark her removal from polite society, completely and utterly, surely. She could not imagine how her life would progress from that point.

She had a little money again, now, with what she had got back from Simeon. She could ask her father to raise a loan and use that to move away. Ann Davenport would surely give up, if Marianne was out of the house. They could leave London and go somewhere cheaper. Head north, perhaps.

But they were still tied as blood relations. Marianne felt pursued, and thought of relentless foxhounds, and tried to put it all out of her mind as she ascended the steps to speak once more to Tobias.

He had relaxed, she found. He was speaking more now,

although it was to Simeon rather than her. She told them both of what had been happening, and advanced her theory about the jewels and the potential whereabouts of Mrs Newman.

"You know that house as well as anyone, Tobias. Where could she be hiding?"

He didn't know exactly where, but he admitted that she could be in there, somewhere.

"There are rooms and cupboards there that have not been opened for years. A hundred years or more. And doors connecting rooms in strange ways. You can go in one room and she will slip out another way, and you could circle one another for hours and never come across her. She need not be hiding in a hole or behind a secret panel." He nearly laughed. "I made it into a game of mine, sometimes. She never found me if I did not want to be found. And the same now goes for her."

"Let me ask you a question, Simeon. It is still preying on my mind about these noises. You are an illusionist. How do you create noise?"

"It depends on the noise. Can you imitate it?"

She threw her voice as high as she could, and made some sing-song screeches.

"No," said Tobias, listening with a certain degree of pain on his face. "It starts almost as if it is speaking. It reminds me of *Mary Had A Little Lamb*."

"I thought of nursery rhymes when I first heard it but I never caught any words," Marianne said.

"It used to be clearer."

"It has deteriorated with time?" Simeon interrupted. "And

there is no kind of phonograph in the place?"

"No," Marianne said, looking to Tobias for confirmation. "No."

"Still, a trick is being played and I would wager if you spent a night there now, you would not hear it – unless you are right, and she is still there, and she wants to scare you away. Look for something that could be a phonograph in disguise."

"If it is in disguise, how would I recognise it?"

Simeon rolled his eyes. "Use your analytical nature," he told her. "How does a phonograph work?"

"A cylinder with grooves in it, and a stylus, and a handle, and a large trumpet to amplify the sound."

"Or a disc. It need not be a cylinder. And it need not be tinfoil. Look also for wax," Simeon told her. "There are remarkable things being invented now. Even the trumpet may not look like a trumpet. Just as that bunch of flowers there looks like a duck."

It was definitely a duck but she believed him anyway.

"I must go there right away," she said, enthused by the new information. "Would you two like to come as well? We could spend the night there, looking for Mrs Newman. Or ghosts. And waiting for the screams."

"That sounds utterly horrid, and no, thank you," Simeon said.

Tobias shook his head too. "I'll not ever step foot there again," he said, and that was that.

***

183

Marianne found Phoebe lying in her bedroom in the dark, curled up on her side under the covers. It was late afternoon.

"Can you talk?" Marianne whispered.

"Come in. The worst is passing. But be gentle."

"Can I fetch anything for you?"

"No, no. Emilia has been a darling."

"She told me about Mrs Cogwell."

"Oh, don't remind me." Phoebe did not even try to sit up. She remained in a foetal position and spoke without opening her eyes. When her headaches came on, only sleep seemed to really help. "I do not know what I'm going to do about that. I have had an actual argument with her – with my mother, I mean. I asked her to leave. She said no. And then I told her to leave. But she won't."

"Why not?"

"Pride. Genuine concern, too. She honestly thinks the household will end up ruined if we continue as we are."

"Financially?"

"In a sense, yes. But she has become so much more religious and she is honestly terrified for the state of our souls. She believes we will burn in hell, and because she loves us, she does not want that."

Marianne winced. "I think she was always religious-minded but it does seem to have overtaken her more lately."

"She is a woman who needs a project, an outlet for her energy. Just like you. You share the same stubbornness and determination."

"Ha. I suppose we ought to have been friends."

"Indeed. So now we must toe the line and live according to our means and present the right sort of modest face to the world, and you, Marianne…"

"Must marry. That's why I've come to see you. You need to organise a dinner party on my behalf, as soon as possible. I will be bringing a guest to totally throw your mother off the scent."

"Are you going to fake a marriage?"

"Fake it? I may even do it, just for the fun of it."

"You would not. Who is it? Simeon – oh, Simeon! That poor boy. But she will recognise him from his appearances here, and he has not made a good impression. I am sure she had ordered him to be shot if he reappears. She won't be convinced and she certainly won't improve."

"You just rest now." Marianne patted her on the shoulder. "I have it in hand."

"What is happening with the case at Rosedene? Is it over?"

"No. And yes. There is more I need to investigate." She thought about her urge to spend the night there. Not tonight, she decided. She was needed here. And she had to portray the part of the dutiful young woman to convince Mrs Davenport that she was mending her ways. "But I'll tell you about it when you feel better."

Phoebe let out a long breath.

Marianne quietly withdrew.

Nineteen

Marianne chafed under the obligations she had placed on herself during the following days. She could not escape the planning and preparation for the dinner party. She wanted to send a message to the police, urging Inspector Gladstone to measure every inch of Rosedene and charting its crevices and nooks on a plan to identify the secret hiding place – or places. Meanwhile, she was stuck at Woodfurlong, and working at Mrs Davenport's every beck and call. She sent out one personal invitation to the dinner party. To her delight, it was accepted.

With the restrictions now enforced on Mrs Cogwell, the preparation of a meal was a much more involved task for Phoebe and she needed Marianne's help. Mrs Cogwell was to leave at the end of the following week, and Phoebe had promised her a glowing character, in spite of Mrs Davenport's threats, and said that would do everything she could to find her a new position. Mrs Davenport had been shocked at the cook's announcement and then chosen to see it as an example of exactly why she could not be trusted. Mrs Davenport said that she was vindicated in her imposition of new rules, and carried a new air of rather unchristian smugness.

Marianne avoided being in her presence as much as possible. She wanted to make a good impression, but it was easier to do that from a distance. If she was near to Mrs Davenport, she was not sure she could hold her tongue under provocation. She took it upon herself to decorate the table and the dining room in general, and was assisted by Emilia who had been reading the very latest advice on such matters. The theme was to be "the seaside" and Marianne was attempting to create a centrepiece out of shells with cascading ferns to look like seaweed.

Phoebe spent most of the day of the dinner party in the kitchen, and took control of the fine sugar-work for the meal, and then the pair of them had the onerous task of changing and preparing themselves for the evening. Emilia came to help Marianne after she had dressed her mistress, and paid particular attention to her hair, concocting a style to hide her forehead as much as possible. "Mrs Davenport says that we are not to hint at intelligence," she said.

Phoebe was already tipsy by the time that Marianne came down to await the arrival of the other guests. Price was in a corner of the room, by the fire, hiding behind a newspaper, and Mrs Davenport was prowling around, criticising everything for either being too showy, or not showy enough.

She descended at last on Marianne, who could not get away any longer. "I am perfectly on edge with excitement, awaiting your beau," she said.

"You must not worry. I have been heeding your advice. I

188

know that you wished to make your own choice for me but..."

"No, no, child! I had no wish at all to impose my views on you! I only insist on your happiness – that is all." She smiled almost as if she meant it.

When Jack arrived, Phoebe greeted him warmly, though she shot a glare of disapproval at Marianne. When Marianne had told her who she was inviting, right at the very last minute, Phoebe had been annoyed.

"He promises not to break into any of your private rooms this time," Marianne had assured her.

Price looked confused at first, but saw that the womenfolk were not making a fuss, and decided that he probably didn't recognise the man after all.

Mr and Mrs Jenkins were likewise perfectly polite.

And Jack turned on every inch of charm for everyone. When he was introduced to Mrs Davenport, his low voice and gentle handshake seemed to make her almost – just almost – giggle.

"Is she simpering?" Marianne hissed to Phoebe.

"My own mother? No! And she is a happily married woman."

"I would wager your father is enjoying every moment of his current freedom."

"No, I should think he is lost without her. All the more reason for your plan tonight to work. I must ask, though, how did you get that man to agree to play along?"

Marianne smiled thinly. "Ah, well, as to that, he does not *entirely* know what he is playing along with."

"Marianne! That is not fair."

"It doesn't matter to him. All I need to do is portray to your mother that I am close to an eligible and decent gentleman. He is good at pretending to be that. She can leap merrily to her own conclusions. But really, he's only here for the food and drink. And perhaps another issue that you can help us with – but I'll talk about that later. He will need your help, Phoebe. Don't breathe a word of my plan to him, though, please."

"But when he finds out? He must find out."

"How can he? It is not as if your mother will whip out a clergyman from a cupboard and demand to see us wed right here, tonight."

"Do not give her ideas. She might. Ah, hello, Mr Monahan, I am so delighted you could join us. I think we are ready to go through…?"

***

Unfortunately, Marianne had underestimated the force of Mrs Davenport's determination to see Marianne wed, and out of her daughter's house. And she had the tact and diplomacy of a brick breaking a window.

Even Mr and Mrs Jenkins, who were uncommonly beige people with no inclination to gossip simply because they were too dull to notice anything worth gossiping about, had begun to shift awkwardly in their seats as Mrs Davenport pressed Jack with questions that were far too personal and very obviously matrimonial in character.

Marianne tried to deflect these probes but she knew she was seeming rude by interrupting, and even Phoebe was growing red in the face as her mother spoke.

"So tell me, dear Mr Monahan, what are your thoughts on servants? If a household of, say, five hundred a year, has a man in livery, what do you make of that?"

"Preposterous, of course," he replied, after sneaking a look at Marianne who was indicating, with her eyebrows, that such a thing was impossible.

"Quite, quite. Those that emphasise only the outward show of things are like gaudy peacocks, useless in society, quite useless. Like the ringing of a hollow bell, one might say. And where do you worship, sir?"

"Um…"

It was the longest dinner party that Marianne had ever endured and she could no longer meet Jack's eye by the end of it. She pretended instead to be a blushing maiden, every time he addressed her, and looked down at her plate.

When the ladies withdrew and left the men alone, Phoebe walked next to Marianne and said in a low voice, "You are looking less and less like a woman in love, you know."

"I think Jack is going to kill me."

"Oh dear; a lover's tiff so soon."

"Don't joke about this, Phoebe. Oh good; some wine."

"Mother will not be pleased if you over-indulge."

"Nothing I do can please her. Anyway, one cannot over-indulge on this lightly-scented water. How far can she possibly water it down?"

"I know. I am sorry," Phoebe said. "I know exactly how it feels. Not the wine, I mean, the feeling that you cannot ever please her."

Marianne was struck suddenly and she stopped. "She is proud of you, I am sure. You are married and have children, after all."

"Oh, yes, I suppose I have done my duty. But she has never once told me that she is proud of me. I shouldn't be upset. I am sorry – your own mother, after all…"

Marianne nodded. She remembered how her father had told her that he thought her mother would have been proud of her, and she kept it to herself. Poor Phoebe. It was not right that Marianne felt more loved by a dead mother, than Phoebe felt by her own living one. She rubbed her cousin's arm. "Wine, then, for both of us. Come on."

The men joined them remarkably quickly, as was the growing fashion, in spite of Mrs Davenport's displeasure. Marianne mingled with Mr and Mrs Jenkins, but Jack hovered nearby, shooting increasingly dangerous looks in her direction. Mrs Jenkins smiled and whispered to Marianne, "I think he desires a private word, my dear. It would not do to play *too* aloof."

Relationship advice from the dullest woman in the county. Marianne grimaced briefly. She excused herself and walked to a closeted corner of the room, away from the fire, where a few chairs were scattered artfully around a circular table. Jack followed, clutching a glass of wine. He set his back to the room so that no one could see his face, and got close as he hissed, "You have let everyone believe we have an understanding, haven't you? I am not even going to ask what is going on – it is plain. You are playing me for a fool!"

"No, Jack, please don't mistake me," she replied. "You and I have both agreed that we are not suited as partners. And I have not forgotten my promise to you."

"Then why this farce?"

"I can explain. Shall we take a turn outside? For the air?"

"I guess, then, that you don't wish to be overheard. Come along. My darling." He extended his arm and she took it. He fixed a wolfish and entirely fake grin on his face and led her out of the drawing room, much to Mrs Davenport's mixed delight and horror. Marianne saw her push Phoebe towards them, probably intending for her to be a chaperone. But Jack walked briskly and the front door was half-open, with Mr Barrington peering out into the night. They slipped past him and turned left, down the stone steps and into a small shrubbery that lay just off the front lawns. The lights on the porch cast enough light for them to see one another.

Marianne rather wished she was in complete darkness.

"I will not lie to you. You are going to think all of this rather trivial, but I assure you, the situation has plunged the entire household into the utmost misery."

He let go of her arm and waited.

She ploughed on with her awkward explanation. "The fact is, Phoebe's mother, that dreadful Mrs Davenport, is set upon my marriage. She will not leave the house until I am betrothed. She is ashamed of me and also fears for my immortal soul, as my single state puts me in too much danger of falling."

He laughed at that.

"Stop it. She's deadly serious. Plus, she is awfully keen on economy being next to Godliness."

"That's cleanliness."

"No, not for her. Living within one's means is some kind of holy grace in her view. And appearing to be what one is not – either higher or lower – is a sin as one is challenging God's allotted order of things. It makes little sense to me. Anyway, she has imposed a tight budget upon this household and I am a drain upon it."

"A budget, you say? Well, that explains the thoroughly rotten wine we have been served. I've passed water with a higher alcohol content."

"I know. It is dreadful. Now, if Mrs Davenport believes I am in with a chance of marriage, she will leave this house. That is all you need to do – just be yourself but do not contradict her assumptions. We need go no further than that."

"I suppose we are playing along by hiding in the shrubbery."

"Yes," Marianne said. "She will be scandalised by the detail but relieved, I think, that it seems I have found a man foolish enough to… sorry. But you know what I mean."

"He would have to be a fool, indeed. No, Marianne. I cannot play along with this."

"Jack! I know I have asked a lot of you lately. And don't fear that I have forgotten my promise to you. When Mrs Davenport has gone from this place, then Phoebe and I can turn our attentions to matchmaking on your behalf."

"Oh. Oh yes, I should never have spoken of that to you."

"Don't be embarrassed!"

"I'm not," he snapped. "But this has gone too far. Do you

know what is annoying me the most?"

"The deception," she said quietly.

"Exactly so. You should have warned me. I feel as if I have been made a fool of."

"You might have refused."

"Perhaps." He turned as if to go. "What a mess. At least the food was good."

"Well, that shan't stay the same for much longer," Marianne told him. "Mrs Cogwell, the cook, is leaving next week."

"What? She is a marvel. Where is she going?"

"I don't know. She has not secured a place yet, so I think she intends to lodge with an aunt in Camberwell."

He sighed. "And if Mrs Davenport can be persuaded to leave very soon?"

"Then Mrs Cogwell can stay. And you can come to dinner any time you please," she added rashly.

"Very well, then. I am defeated. I am doing this only for the sake of fresh scallops and divine blancmange. And I may be a fool, but I am no quitter. Oh, Marianne, I will laugh about this, in a few years' time. Come, then. Would you take my arm, *my dear?*"

"Gladly."

They waltzed out of the shrubbery and towards the stone steps of the porch. The door had been left ajar just a little. As they began to ascend the steps, Marianne stopped and turned to look down the gravel drive. She could hear feet crunching and they were coming quickly.

A running figure shot out of the darkness and raced up the

steps, his hair and clothing flapping and his breath rasping painfully.

"Simeon! Stop," she cried, pulling free of Jack's grasp and jumping up to the top step to intercept her friend. "What's happened? Have a care; the staff have been warned about you, now."

"Let him get his breath back," Jack told her.

They persuaded Simeon to sit on the top step and get himself under control. When he was able to speak, he blurted out, "They've arrested Tobias!"

"No. Who? The police?"

"Of course the police! They came – maybe an hour ago, must be more – I ran all the way here – I could not think – he's going to hang for murder!"

"He cannot."

"He's the only one who benefited from that old lady's death. He is known to be strange."

"No he's not," Marianne protested. "How does a limp and a silent attitude make one strange?"

Jack said, "Such things are said to be a mark of a criminal mind."

"What nonsense. He is a poor young boy, alone in the world."

"And likely unhinged. That will be his best defence, according to the police," Simeon said. "They were gentle with him. They said he ought to claim madness and spend his days in an asylum."

"This is a travesty. I knew Inspector Gladstone was under

pressure but this is a boy's whole life that hangs in the balance."

"Hangs," said Jack. "Good pun. Do you see?"

"Not now. *Dear heart*," she added hastily as Mrs Davenport came out of the house, attracted by the noise. "Simeon, run, hide!"

"What?"

Marianne pushed at him and he stumbled down the steps while Mr Barrington, quickly weighing up the situation, got Mrs Davenport's attention on him. "Madam, please do watch your step. Here, take my arm if you will." She turned her head to the steward, and Simeon ran off into the darkness.

"Good heavens. What is occurring here?" Mrs Davenport said, staring hard at Marianne and Jack. "You should come back inside at once."

"Of course. Do forgive me." Marianne glanced at Jack, who was still looking faintly exasperated at the ongoing charade. He offered his arm once more, and they followed Mrs Davenport back into the house.

As soon as they were in the hall, and Mrs Davenport was sailing towards the stairs to ascend to the drawing room, Marianne wrestled herself free of Jack's grasp. "I am so sorry," she said quietly. "I will be back in just a moment. I need to check that Simeon is all right. Um, Jack, do you have any money?"

His hand patted his jacket. "Yes, thank you."

"Might I borrow a few coins so that I can send Simeon back to his rooms?"

"Good heavens. We are not even married yet, and you are already bleeding me dry."

"Jack! He can pay you back, I know it. He has the money that you got him from those brothers. Who aren't brothers. But I know Simeon very well. He will have not thought to bring anything with him. He has panicked, and he has run."

"If we must perform this tedious pantomime, allow me to play my *full* part," he said, and slipped her a little money. "Now go, but I shall not be able to hold her off for long; she will soon notice your absence."

Marianne paused, then smiled, warmly and genuinely. "Thank you. Thank you; I really mean it."

He pushed her. "Go!"

She dashed past the bemused-looking Mr Barrington and out into the night once more.

Twenty

Simeon was crouching in the shrubbery where she had been talking with Jack. The light from the porch was filtered through the branches and falling leaves, casting black and orange blobs over his face.

"Here," she said. "Take this money. It will be enough to get you home."

"But what about Tobias?"

"I will speak to Inspector Gladstone in the morning," she assured him. "But as you can see, I'm rather stuck here at the moment. And they will not hang him overnight. There will be a trial and so on. Except it won't come to that, once I speak to the Inspector."

"What can the Inspector do? What can anyone do?" Simeon wailed. He clutched at his head. She could see he was heading into one of his attacks. If he had been a woman, they would have called him hysterical. "Oh, is it my fault? I could have hidden him. I should have hidden him!"

She reached out and patted him. He sank slowly to his knees and she followed him down, slightly awkwardly. The hem of her dress was in the earth and wet leaves. The maids were going to be furious. She would owe them a stint by the copper come Monday, the habitual wash-day.

He rocked forwards and ended up with his head buried in her shoulder. She embraced him and soothed him like he was a child. "You trusted me," he was moaning softly. "I let you down…"

"Mari-ANNE."

The high pitched wail of Mrs Davenport split the dark night. Marianne jerked, but held on to the trembling Simeon. She turned to see the shadowy outline of Mrs Davenport, haloed all around by the porch lamps. But she didn't need to see her face to know that it would be utterly appalled by what she could make out.

Mr Barrington came to Mrs Davenport's side with a lamp in his hand. There was nowhere for Marianne to hide.

At first she thought that the main problem was simply Simeon's interruption to the dinner party. She patted his shoulder again as she stood up and said, "Do not be alarmed. It's just that my friend Simeon has had a terrible shock."

"That person cannot be your friend. Your betrothed is inside. Marianne, this is debauchery of the very lowest sort and I can only imagine what scandal is already brewing in the minds of our guests. If you come inside now, we can possibly redeem this whole shocking situation."

"There is no hint of a scandal here," she protested even as she knew, very well, that women had been ruined for less. Squatting in a shrubbery with another man? Mrs Davenport was quite correct. It was almost insurmountable.

"Marianne, please," Mrs Davenport snapped. "Do not make this worse. Our dinner party guests are inside and you have a duty. Come inside. Let Barrington expel that person. And he is lucky to escape with his life. He ought to be whipped from the property."

"He will not!" she said.

"Marianne! I counsel you very strongly against such insubordination. You are so very close to the line."

Marianne took the decision to dance right over that line. "You are not my mother," she spat out, knowing such a terrible sentence made her sound quite young and petty and did nothing for creating an impression of dignity.

"I might not be, but I stand here in her stead, and…"

"Actually, you do not."

Mrs Davenport gaped and stopped talking as Russell spoke behind her, in the strong voice of a man much younger. He must have awoken and come out from his rooms in search of the leavings of the dinner party meal. It was nearly nine o'clock now. He was followed by everyone else: Price, Phoebe, Mr and Mrs Jenkins, and of course, Jack, who was watching proceedings with amusement.

"What on earth gives you the right to upbraid my own daughter, you vile old hag?"

Mrs Davenport quivered with indignation. "How dare you! I have my God-given right to see all of His flock cleave to the straight and narrow path."

"You are a hypocrite of the very highest order, standing there in your mixed fabrics, with your unceasing attention to how you might be seen in society, your vanity and vainglorious nature, your showy charity, your shallow and flimsy faith, a thing of no substance but that which seems to show you as a righteous person as if you can get to the Kingdom of Heaven by blatant outward deeds, all the while trumpeting your own Christian nature."

Everyone fell still and silent. He addressed them with the gravity and conviction of one born in a pulpit of fire and brimstone, and Marianne was amazed. Maybe he hadn't been asleep during any of her long conversations and rants after all. Phoebe had emerged behind Russell, the lights of the hallway throwing an angel-like aura around her. She put a hand to her mouth and watched her mother's reaction warily.

For Mrs Davenport was not a bad person, not really, thought Marianne. Annoying, infuriating, misguided and yes – vain in the strangest of ways. But she didn't actively set out to be any of those things. Who did?

She could see that Phoebe's loyalties were being torn in two.

Simeon quivered and stood up unsteadily. He whispered to Marianne, "I must go. I am so sorry."

"I'm coming with you," she announced, loudly.

"I should not have come."

"You did exactly the right thing." She faced the assembled onlookers who were crowding at the top step. "I have a real and important *role*," she said proudly. "A *job* which I intend to do. I am sorry, but *business* calls me away from this otherwise enjoyable meal. If my *intended* can understand this, then so can all of you. Thank you." Her heart was pounding with the illogical fear and anxiety that speaking out brought; it was silly to be scared of speaking like this to people one knew, but she felt it anyway. Then she caught sight of her father and he was miming applause. She flashed him a quick smile.

Mrs Davenport looked pale and shaky, as if she was going to faint – a real one, not a fake Mrs Newman kind of flutter. Mr Barrington was at her side instantly. Phoebe took a step towards Marianne.

"No, you have a duty here," she said to her cousin. "You must stay. Please look after your mother."

"Where are you going? You cannot go!"

"I am clearly not welcome here any longer. I suppose that I am ruined anyway. I am so sorry…"

She turned around and walked down the steps with Simeon hunched at her side. He had stopped muttering now. She knew he was frozen into silence by the heaps of guilt he would currently be piling onto his own head. She whispered, "It will all turn out for the best. Let us just get to your rooms."

He didn't reply but she took it as agreement.

A moment later she heard footsteps crunching on the gravel. It was Jack, catching her up, with his outdoor coat slung over his arm.

"I rather think that you both need escorts at this time of night," he said. "Keep walking. Stay warm. But I have asked for my gig to be made ready; I will go back and assist, and then catch you up. Stay on the road."

"Thank you. I don't know what to say."

He shrugged. "It will give them all a little more to gossip

203

about. I have no reputation to sully anyway. On you go." He darted back to the house and the stables.

She realised she had not returned the money that she had borrowed. She patted her purse. She would have to remember to give it back.

Marianne took Simeon's arm and they pressed on until Jack came by and wedged them all, most tightly and uncomfortably, into the tiny gig, and the horse strained on into the ever-busy streets of the city.

***

Once at the workshop, she thanked Jack over and over and then urged him to go home, which he did willingly. She helped Simeon up the rickety steps to his rooms. She had nothing but her good dinner party dress and impractical shoes, and her father remained at Woodfurlong. She had completed her public fall from grace into shame and ignominy. Marianne began to feel nervous.

But also very, very tired. She was, really, relieved to be away from Woodfurlong, and worried for her father, and cross with Gladstone for arresting Tobias, and annoyed generally at the whole mess of a situation that she was embroiled in.

Then she thought, I ought to be grateful for this. At least life is interesting. It might end up being short – what with all these ruffians and threats of whippings and what not – but no one can say that I didn't make the most of it. I am doomed anyway, almost utterly ruined, a spinster and most unnatural –

why not pursue adventure?

"You're smiling in a sinister way," Simeon said, fumbling with his key. "Don't. This whole thing is just a mess without that."

"I know. I am sorry to have brought all this on you. I am so tired."

"Oh – oh no. I don't have a spare bed. I will take the sofa," he muttered as they went into the freezing cold workshop. He flapped around, and she let him be in motion, as it seemed to calm him down to be moving and active. Within fifteen minutes, she was tucked up under layers and layers of blankets with a hot brick wrapped in cloth at her feet, and Simeon was already snoring in the next room.

At least he could sleep.

She said another prayer of gratitude, and fell asleep herself.

Twenty-one

She woke up. It was very early and she had not had enough sleep, but she was itching to get on with things. Everything had to be made right, somehow. The events of the previous night were already a blur with sharp edges of pain when she recalled certain things that had been said or done.

She had thought, last night, that her fall from polite society must be complete and irreversible now. This morning, she wondered if that were true. Perhaps it was not the end for her. She had to act as if she had a future. The world was changing every year, every month. Perhaps it could change to accommodate her.

She listened but could not hear anything but Simeon's light breathing and occasional dry snores, so she wrapped a blanket around herself and peeped through the door. Simeon was sprawled on the floor although whether that was by choice or accident, she could not tell. Otherwise, the place was empty. The high windows let in a greyish light. She padded around silently, found some cold water, and took it back to the other room for a wash. It wasn't really a bedroom except that it had Simeon's bed in it. There were also mirrors and springs and boxes of ribbons and a stuffed parrot in an elaborate cage. It wasn't a spacious set of rooms but it was unusual for London. She cast her mind back to how Judy was living, in one pokey closet down that smelly side street. And she was lucky to have her own bed, though it was just a plank of wood.

Marianne hoped that would not be her own future.

When she came back out again, cleaner and dressed in a presentable way, Simeon was awake too. He had slept in his clothes, and he did not smell fresh.

"How are you feeling today?" she asked. She opened the main door onto the wooden steps, and looked down into the street which was teeming with life. It was a sea of moving black and grey and blue, just hats and umbrellas making an almost unbroken platform. She fancied she could jump down and walk across the street at head height.

"Full of regret."

"That's how most people wake up once they become adults."

"Ha. It doesn't seem real. What are you going to do?"

"Have breakfast," she said.

"I have bread that isn't totally mouldy."

"How tempting. And coffee?"

"Possibly. The fire will take a little while to light. There is something blocking the chimney."

"Maybe one of your doves got away."

"Don't joke," he said quietly as he began to rattle around with pots and pans. "It could be poor Bonny, up there."

While he got on with preparing a rudimentary and hopefully

edible breakfast, Marianne paced the workshop.

"What is your plan?" he asked.

"I have in mind an awful lot of burglary," she confessed.

"Because you are not in enough trouble already?"

"We need to unearth Mrs Newman out of that house. She is the only key to saving Tobias. And consequently clearing my name."

"How does that clear your name?"

"Well, it probably doesn't," she said. "But it makes enough of a good name for me, that it might overshadow the bad. And you know, I think there may be a positive in all of this. Now I am out of Woodfurlong, Mrs Davenport has no reason to continue residing there and plaguing the staff. She has taught Phoebe household management, she has pared down the number of servants by at least one, and she has ejected me. I am concerned for my father but she surely cannot force him out, too. Price and Phoebe must step in on his behalf."

"And once she has left, you can go back?"

"I don't want to return until I have covered myself in glory and solved this case. Then I can go back in triumph and not as a slatternly floozy with no morals and low standards."

"Because if people think you are carrying on with me, that shows your low standards?" Simeon said. "Oh, I am sorry for how it turned out."

"I know, you said. Repeatedly. But we must move on," Marianne said as decisively as possible.

"On to this housebreaking plan of yours."

"Well," she said. "The first place I need to access is not so much a house of residence…"

***

It was nearly midnight. She had spent the day preparing and taking little naps, practising her lock-picking and running through the order of planned events. Now she was about to do it. She was accompanied by Simeon, who was a quivering ball of terror and panic, but he was hiding it fairly well and trying to seem strong for her sake.

He had been sent out earlier that day to perform a specific task down Albemarle Street. She needed one pane of glass to be broken in the sash window near the door. It would not be large enough for them to crawl through, but that did not matter. It just needed to be broken. It had taken a lot to persuade him to go out and throw the stone. In the end, she had used the money that she still had in her possession from Jack, and told Simeon to pay a street urchin to perform the necessary vandalism. He came home almost silent, and she felt bad for asking him to do it, but it would make their evening escapade a lot easier.

Albemarle Street was quiet. Who wanted to browse along the art galleries and auction houses at this time of night? Over the road, theatre-goers left their palaces of entertainment and hailed cabs and carriages. Men stalked the streets and painted women cooed to them from corners. Policemen walked their set beats, and young boys and girls slipped from shadow to shadow, looking for food, or money, or chances, or just somewhere safe to sleep for a few cold hours.

She was dressed in an odd combination of clothes. She had not dared to go back to Woodfurlong to gather up any of her things, not yet. She would have to, soon. She had sent a message to her father assuring him that she was fine and unharmed, but she had not received a reply. If Mrs Davenport had intercepted it, then Marianne felt a surge of violent action coming on. She squashed that thought. Not even Mrs Davenport was that cruel. So she still wore her fine gown from the dinner party, but with a long dark cloak from the supply that Simeon had kept in a cupboard. When he had been performing on stage, he had been assisted by a variety of women. From that same stock, she had borrowed some soft-soled shoes to change into, and a dark cloth to wrap around her hair. A hat would be too easily knocked off and she could not risk her hair tumbling down.

From some distance away, she could see that the broken pane of glass had been replaced with a rectangle of wood as a temporary measure. It would not have mattered if it had been glass, because the putty would have been fresh enough to let them pull the pane out safely. The wood was just as easily removed. There was quarter-moon moulding holding the wood in place, with a scattering of thin panel pins, and they were easily prised out. She worked slowly, stopping to listen. There would surely be a night-watchman within, and she had chosen the window far away from any desks and offices deliberately.

The gap was large enough for her head but nothing more. That did not matter. She poked her head in cautiously. There was a faint light far at the end of the entrance hall, showing a glow from around a corner. She turned to look at the window

211

frame. She'd noted the alarm system on her previous visit, and now she could have a better look at it.

She grinned. It wasn't a modern one. This was one of Pope or Holmes's original inventions from back in the fifties. There would be no telegraphic communication to alert anyone of the window opening. All she had to do was concentrate on keeping the circuit open so that the bell on this window would not ring. Each door and window had its own little system, its own battery, and its own electro-magnet.

It was rather ingenious and so simple. If the sash window was raised, a piece of foil on the window edge would slide over two metal contacts and complete the circuit. The flow of current would trigger the electro-magnet to exert its mysterious force on a spring-loaded armature and that would strike the bell, bringing the night-watchman out to investigate.

Ideally, they would have built that system right into the wooden frame of the sash mechanism but that was a lot of effort, and hard to maintain. So it was a clumsy affair tacked on to the side of the window. She followed the wire and found the gap. She had a very thin slice of polished bone that Simeon used in his tricks. She knew that it would not conduct electricity and she hoped that the window would still move, sliding over the wafer-thin hard surface. She pushed it into place, and it wedged firmly. Then she withdrew her head and listened for any footsteps.

Nothing.

Steadily, silently, Marianne and Simeon pressed thin wooden wedges beneath the lower edge of the sash window. Metal would have been easier but she didn't want to risk touching any wires.

They had to angle the points down and then lever upwards, very slowly. The window rose a touch and then touched the thin bone strip. It stopped.

She breathed in, breathed out, counted to three and nodded to Simeon. They increased the pressure. It jammed, shuddered, and then – with a tiny cracking sound – continued upwards.

No bell sounded.

They lifted the sash only as far as they needed to be able to wriggle in. Simeon propped it with a block of wood. Again they waited to see if they had made too much noise.

The watchman, wherever he was in the building, was not alerted to their presence. She tapped Simeon on the shoulder, and slipped into the hushed, cathedral-like reception area of the auction house. He waited outside.

She had to discover two things. One was where the night-watchman habitually placed himself, which she assumed was in the direction of the pale light, and two was where the notebook would be kept. She assumed it would be with the jewels, and therefore the jewels would be locked in a box or safe of some kind. Therefore there had to be an inventory system. Rather than open boxes at random, she went straight to the main desk and began to search through the ledgers. She pulled them to the floor and crouched down, hidden by the wooden desk, keeping her ears strained for the sound of anyone approaching. She fumbled for her lucifers and lit a candle to read by.

The first ledger was a record of transactions. She put it quietly to one side and turned to the next, and the next. Finally she found what she was looking for. The paper rustled under her fingers and she moved as slowly and silently as possibly, hunting down the list of "assets received" until she spotted Miss Dorothea Newman recorded in the "original owner" column.

Footsteps approached. She licked her fingers and pinched out the candle stub, cupping her hand over the wick as it smoked. She stopped moving and almost stopped breathing, staying hunched down in the space between the stools and the desk.

The man passed by without even slowing or pausing, and a door closed at the far end of the hall.

She resumed her scrutiny of the ledger with the candle freshly lit. There was a code next to the description of the items and it was easy to understand that "R1B27" was going to be room one, box twenty-seven. She carefully replaced the ledgers and slid out into the hall. She glanced in the direction that the watchman had gone. The door was closed. The pale light had disappeared.

So she passed through to the display rooms at the rear, and spotted what she had overlooked on her first visit: numbered side-rooms. She found room one, and had picked the lock within a minute.

Thank goodness for the hours of practise she'd put in that day, while Simeon had been out breaking windows.

She stepped into the small room and pulled the door closed behind her. There were no windows to the main display area, and the room itself was small and dark, lit by a skylight which of course showed nothing. She wedged the stub of a candle on the central circular table and squinted into the dancing shadows. The walls were lined with small boxes. So, she guessed, the other rooms held larger items, sculptures, paintings. Room one was for small things. Now she needed a large dose of luck.

She found box number twenty-seven marked by a brass nameplate. She pulled it out and it slid easily, being made of polished wood resting on a wooden shelf, and it seemed light. She carried it to the candle and examined the lock.

It was complicated.

She was not going to be able to pick it; she knew it even as soon as she started to probe into it. She could spend the night here and get nowhere. She straightened up and thought deeply. Could she break into it? Not without a great deal of noise.

So she would have to take it with her.

The idea filled her with dread. She only wanted the notebook, not the jewels. Somehow, stealing actual jewellery felt like a step too far. But she vowed that she would return them and perhaps even manage to do that secretly. There was a chance that no one would ever know what she had done here.

Oh well, she told herself, faking confidence. In for a penny, in for a pound. She used one of her lock-picking tools to unscrew the nameplate and she went to the far end of the shelves and found a blank, empty box. This one was shabby and scuffed, and there was a mark where the original nameplate had been removed. She screwed the small rectangle into place and put the empty box in the gap where the original had been. It would not stand up to scrutiny but it was less eye-catching than a gap.

She extinguished the candle, waited for the top of it to harden slightly, and shoved the squidgy lump into her bag of tools. With the box under her arm, and her bag in her hand, she only had one hand free. She took a deep breath, cracked open the door, waited and listened, and finally, heart thumping, slithered out through the display hall, through the main reception room, and back to the window.

Simeon's face was a pale white oval with huge terrified eyes. She passed him the box and her bag, and he dumped them on the street while she slithered through the crack. They pulled out the block of wood and carefully lowered the sash. She removed the bone shard, nearly dropping it which made her heart thud, and then they replaced the wood in the window.

The only thing that they could not do was hammer the thin nails back in.

They did their best to push the panel pins into the previous holes, using the wooden block to add pressure. It was an unsatisfactory job but they could not hang about. With every moment, they risked discovery. Simeon had not seen any policemen which meant it was growing more and more likely that one would pass on their regular beat.

They picked up their items, and fled.

Twenty-two

"I cannot keep taking your bed," she said, once they were back in his rooms.

Simeon waved her objection away. "I am not going to sleep tonight. After everything that has happened, I feel too full of … something. Electricity, maybe! I will work, instead."

"You must sleep! Do not make yourself ill on my account."

"Oh, no. It's on my own account. I slept heavily last night and my dreams were troubling. I think that tonight, I will fight the demons while I am awake. It is easier that way."

"No, Simeon…"

"Hush," he said. All his earlier panic and fear had dissipated, at least on the surface. She marvelled at his ability to oscillate so wildly between states. Now he appeared to be his old self once more. "We have spoken about what we might need to make. Leave the notebook with me. I will read it, and see what I might conjure up for you. Now we have the jewellery too, it changes the possibilities. Meanwhile, you rest. I will sleep tomorrow, in the daylight, when they cannot get me."

She didn't ask who "they" were. It was probably for the

best. She was dog-tired, weary in every heavy limb, and her body obeyed his order to sleep even if her soul and mind protested.

***

The secret was revealed.

Marianne had only slept for five hours and she woke while it was still dark outside. She could hear snoring from the other room. So much for Simeon's plan to work all night, then. She rose and washed in some cold water, left out from the previous day, and wrapped a cloak around the long linen shift that was doing double-duty as a nightshirt. The workshop rooms were terribly cold and she put her fur-lined boots on. She held the cloak tightly around her body and slipped through to the other room. Simeon was full dressed and sprawled in an armchair, asleep. The notebook was on a table next to him, by a low-burning lamp threatening to go out. She adjusted the wick, and took both the lamp and the book to a window overlooking the street where at least some of the gas light was filtering through the grimy glass. She made herself comfortable and plunged into the strange, mad world of the Newman family.

The notebook started as the journal of Mrs Newman.

But Marianne had to backtrack as, after a few pages, she realised this was not the Mrs Newman that she had met. The dates were wrong and she referred to her husband, Mr Arthur Newman. She knew that the Mrs Louisa Newman that she was searching for was married to a man called Cecil. And then she saw that name, and realised she was reading the occasional diary and record-book of Cecil's mother. That would be the current Mrs Louisa Newman's mother-in-law.

Cecil's mother turned out to be Mrs Eglantine Newman, and she lived in Rosedene with her husband Arthur, and Arthur's spinster sister – the late Dorothea Newman. And a child was born: Cecil.

Mrs Eglantine Newman only wrote about large events in her life. This was no journal of the minutiae of everyday life. Marianne was grateful for that. She hadn't wanted to wade through fifty years of what they had had for dinner, and who had said what to whom, and so on.

There was another Mr Newman, the brother of Arthur and Dorothea. He went off to make his fortune, married, had a son called William, who went and had his own family. She put that out of her mind as irrelevant but she was soon flipping back the pages again to try to join the dots.

Because she had reached the point where Cecil had come of age, and married Louisa, bringing it almost up to date.

And goodness, but his parents did *not* agree with the match one bit. Marianne was surprised the paper had not burst into flames, such was the scorn of Eglantine Newman about her son and his proposed bride. But he was in love, and would not be gainsaid, and off they went in secret to be wed.

Oh dear.

And then came the mention of something unusual: "Arthur will not let the Newman Set pass to down to Cecil and his trollop. He is quite, quite sure that Cecil is dead to us now. As for me, there is still time. If he will drop that woman, then all can be as it ought to have been…"

But there seemed to be no chance of that. Determined to make his own name, Cecil and Louisa Newman went to America. The loss of her son overseas seemed to have caused a change of heart in his mother. Now her tone began to soften.

"The Newman Set is supposed to go now to William and his wife, and she is a good woman, and their son Tobias young and strong. But if Cecil would only come back to us… I am stalling Arthur. I must put him off…"

Eventually Eglantine acted. She recorded that "I sent word to Cecil in deepest secrecy. Oh, Arthur cannot know how much my heart breaks for my son. I am afraid he is in dreadful poverty. If he can come back to England, he can find the Set in the place he loved to play as a child. Many hours he spent exploring the secret compartments of that bed. He will know what I mean if I simply say it is in his childhood castle of dreams."

Then a thick black line was drawn under the text, and the handwriting changed. It became small, crabby and hard to read. Marianne was squinting at it in the growing dawn light when Simeon woke up.

He coughed and sniffed and said, from his nest in the armchair, "Have you got to the secret cabinet in the bed part?"

"Yes, I've just read that. But who is the second author of this journal?"

"Oho – keep going. No, I'll tell you. It's Dorothea Newman."

"Ah. And she is writing this recently, even in the past year. Yes, she mentions Tobias coming to stay. And the arrival of Mrs Louisa Newman! Oh, she is not happy about her."

"She uses terrible language for an old lady."

"She was old enough to say whatever she pleased." Marianne read on while Simeon set about brewing some coffee. Right at the end, Dorothea recorded her intentions. "So the Newman Set must be sold on behalf of the boy and the boy alone. He misses school. And she will never have them. Never."

That was it. But they knew the rest.

Marianne stretched and stood up. "Why, then, does Mrs Newman remain in that house?"

"It is obvious."

Marianne nodded, though she was facing away from him and looking out of the window. "Indeed. She has never read this book. She does not know it exists. She does not know that the jewels, the Newman Set, have been removed. She knows that *they* exist and she knows they ought to have passed to Cecil when they were married. Her husband must have told her all that. She must have seen the note that Cecil's mother sent to him – telling him they were hidden. But not where. And Cecil died before he could explain the cryptic family secret – his place of childhood dreams, his castle. To a small boy, that ancient bed would have been another country."

Simeon left the water to come to the boil, and went to the box – or what remained of it, after they had smashed it to pieces to get at the contents. "They are rather gaudy."

"But worth a great deal of money. With the sale of Rosedene, and these jewels, Tobias will be set up for life."

"What little there remains of it."

"Hush now. We will bring this to an end – and soon."

221

***

Marianne went out that morning, her evening gown hidden under the large cloak, and used the last of the money she had borrowed from Jack to buy herself a plain, serviceable dark gown in shades of brown, and a decent bonnet. Gloves were expensive and she was wearing some that she found in Simeon's chest of stage costumes. The air was chilly and the fog was coming down, settling in her chest and making her cough. She could keep the cloak pulled tight around herself in such weather, and she didn't look too out of place in the mass of variety that thronged London's streets. She wouldn't have been able to walk through a village square without attracting notice, but the city was a world of its own.

She went first to Inspector Gladstone, who was busy in a meeting, but one of his policemen told her where she might find Tobias and led her down to the cells himself. She was not allowed in, and not allowed to be alone, but she was able to call through the bars. Half a dozen men were all together in the dark, smelly room. One of them cuffed Tobias on the back of the head, laughing, shoving him forward to the bars of the door.

"Are you all right? Have they harmed you?" she asked.

He spoke in a very low voice. "They have not. One or two of them, they look after me, on account of..." and he indicated his injured leg. "They're not such bad men. They have stories. But ... what is going to happen to me?"

"I've come to tell you not to worry," she told him, firmly.

"I am going to get you released from here."

"Now?" he cried in delight.

Her heart broke, just a little. "No, but soon. Just as soon as we can. So do not lose hope."

She had to leave before she lost control of herself. She could not bear to see him in that vile, filthy place. The policeman was almost smiling at her distress as he led her away and said, "Well, miss, but what did you expect it to be like?"

***

When she got back to Simeon's place, she was surprised and delighted to find Phoebe there.

"Have you come alone?" Marianne cried, rushing into her cousin's embrace.

"I did!" Phoebe said, her eyes wide. "It was such a thrill! I told Emilia and Mr Barrington where I was going but I have sworn them to utmost secrecy unless I do not return home by this evening. Then they may raise any alarm that they see fit. But yes, I travelled on the train alone and I walked through the streets alone, like any common woman!"

She was dressed in dowdy clothing, and Marianne approved until she realised that Phoebe had actually borrowed her own travelling jacket. But she pushed that aside when Phoebe unwrapped the package she had brought with her.

"I thought you would need clothes so – Simeon, look away! These are ladies' things! – so I have brought as much as I could find. Emilia and Nettie helped."

"Oh, thank you!" Marianne scooped up the bundle of necessary items and took them off to the room she had now commandeered as her own bedroom. When she came back out, feeling a great deal fresher and more comfortable, Simeon was bringing some cups of tea over on a tray.

"How is my father?"

"He is utterly livid. He has had to be sedated. Mrs Crouch called for a doctor."

"Oh my. Oh, I am so sorry to have brought all of this down at your door, Phoebe. You too, Simeon. I feel as if I have wrought a trail of disaster that has affected everyone I care about."

"You are totally and utterly the most strong and moral and upright and perfectly *correct* person that I know," Phoebe said, sitting close to her and patting her hands. "Believe that. I support you completely and so does everyone else." She paused, and glared at Simeon until he stammered out, "Oh, yes, we do."

"You see?" Phoebe went on. "So, what is your plan to make it all straight again?"

Marianne nearly laughed with exhaustion and confusion and anxiety. "Oh, the usual," she said, artificially light. "A fake séance. It worked last time, after all."

Phoebe frowned. "It did, but that was a totally different situation. I had an idea, you know." She looked down coquettishly.

"What is it?"

Phoebe giggled. "Oh, it's silly."

"Fair enough, I shan't ask."

"Oh, play the game!"

Marianne sighed wearily. "Please, please, please tell me your wonderful idea."

"We set the house on fire and she *has* to come out into the open."

"Er – no. We cannot do that. That's Tobias's legacy; if it is destroyed, he gets nothing."

"No, I should say, we simply pretend. Simeon can do it. Don't they make artificial smoke in the theatres? Don't they conjure up fire and flames on the stage? If she hears the crackle and she smells the smoke, surely she won't risk being burned to death."

Simeon said, "We could do that. With time. It is not something I have done but I know people who can do it."

Marianne nodded. "We could. But I have a much better idea that is far more certain to work, and will also confirm exactly why I think Mrs Newman remains hiding in Rosedene."

"Which is?"

"She thinks the jewels are still hidden there. We shall demonstrate to her that they are, and she will seek them out, and we will catch her red-handed. All will fall into place."

"And we will use the real jewels?" Simeon asked, nodded at the shards of wood around the bag of jewellery.

"Not … not exactly," Marianne replied. "This part is down to you, Simeon. Phoebe, we shall need your help again, if you would. How would you like to play the part of a medium once more?"

"I'd be delighted," she replied, bouncing up and down.

"And we need one more," Marianne said. "If he is still

willing to talk to me."

"Jack Monahan?"

"The same. And once this is over, we must find him a suitable wife."

Phoebe shook her head. "Now we are straying into fantasies and impossible dreams," she said. She stood up and gathered her things. "I should go home. They will miss me although I have let it be known I have a headache and am not to be disturbed. My mother probably thinks I have said it just to escape from her."

"She is still there?" Marianne asked, getting up to help Phoebe with her cloak.

"She is."

"I thought she would leave now I am gone."

"She plans to … just as soon as she has, in her words, made everything straight."

"Dear God. Will she never go? The only option left is poison, isn't it?"

Phoebe gripped Marianne's forearms tightly, and said in a fierce voice, "Yes. Just a little. But, yes."

Twenty-three

"It is very much based on the same thing that I was making for those Clay brothers," Simeon told her that evening as they dined on jellied eels and brown, lumpy bread soaked in a broth that the street seller had assured them was "beef". There was a fishy taint to it, and it wasn't due to the eels, which were perfect.

Marianne grinned as she watched him demonstrate the workings of the small cabinet.

"It is exactly what I had hoped for," she said with glee.

It was a wooden box, about three inches high and polished to let it slide without anything snagging. The bed in the Grand Bedroom was close to the floor but there was a gap. The box would be pushed far underneath, far enough to be out of sight. Projecting from the top edge was a long thin wooden strip, much like a ruler but with a groove in it, and with a piece of metal at the end. This would be hidden from view and only found by a finger-tip search.

When the metal square was depressed with enough force, it would release a catch in the box, revealing a very strong magnet. The box would move – rather quickly, unfortunately, with no way of slowing it down – firing along the grooved wooden strip to reveal itself as it shot out from underneath the bed. It would trap unwary fingers, but that was unavoidable.

When the box was opened, it would reveal the jewels.

This was their sticking point, and the exercise which took them most of the day. Marianne had not wanted to have the jewels on show. She insisted that Simeon explore ways of projecting the image of the jewels, using mirrors, just like she had seen in the theatre.

It was not possible. Not at such a short distance. "This is *stage* trickery," he had said, over and over. "At close quarters, it is obvious. And I would need a strong light, and more depth to the box, for anything like Pepper's Ghost."

So the real, actual jewellery would be laid in the box, which made her profoundly uneasy. Opening the box primed the system of thin wires. The act of reaching in and taking them would unleash a snare to snap around the wrist. At this point, the person would be stuck fast, at least to the box. Marianne wanted some kind of net to fall from the ceiling, too, but that was also vetoed by Simeon.

"By this point, we will be in the room," he had argued.

"We will be rushing through the house." The séance had to take place in another part of the house, and various other elaborate plays had to be acted out – or Mrs Newman would never be convinced.

"We can do it."

"We will need Jack." And once more she got up and paced through the room, staring out of the window for a messenger bringing a reply to her note.

The infuriating man was certainly making her sweat.

***

In the end, her impatience got the better of her. Now dressed in more comfortable, everyday clothing, she set forth out into the late afternoon. She was equipped to go straight on to Rosedene if possible, to set the trap before they conducted the séance itself. She had the cabinet, the jewels, and a terrifying feeling of impending disaster making butterflies dance in her stomach.

There was so much that could go wrong, not least the fact that she was in the crime-filled London streets hiding valuable trinkets about her person.

Immediately, she was accosted by street food vendors. At this time of day, the streets were busy with workers rushing home, and it was a popular time to buy food. The crowd around her was heading to the nearest railway station and the crush was immense as people fought to leave the city and she had to push against the flow. She bought as much food as she could get for a farthing and ate in a quiet corner, screened by a fancy column, and hoped that no one of importance saw her eating so publicly.

"Good evening. You have pie juice on your chin."

"Jack." She dabbed at her face with her glove. "Ugh."

"When did I stop being Mr Monahan?"

She was surprised but she hoped she didn't show it. She'd called him Jack in her head since she had met him. "I – don't recall. Forgive me."

"No, no. I like it. You've missed a bit. Here." He took a monogrammed handkerchief from his waistcoat pocket and wiped her cheek. She tried not to recoil, and accepted his ministrations as mutely as a child being fussed by a nurse.

"Are you fallen back into your old habit of stalking me?" she asked, trying to sound annoyed.

"Actually no. Although that was fun, wasn't it? No; I have received your note and I was on my way to see you."

"Oh, thank goodness."

"It was somewhat cryptic. Shall we return to Simeon's place, and you can tell me all about it?"

"No," she said. "In fact, I am on my way to Rosedene right now, and I hope you can accompany me."

"Ah, more breaking and entering," he said, falling into step alongside her.

"Only partly so. As a matter of fact, I have a key," she said. "And I will give it to you when we get there. As for me, I shall indeed be breaking in."

"This sounds to be a curious adventure indeed. And the purpose of all this?"

"To lay the groundwork for tomorrow's séance, of course."

"Oh, not again."

"Yes, again. And I should be delighted if you would be one of our guests."

He groaned. "Why do I agree to be mixed up in all of this?"

"Because we are to find you a wife!"

"Hmm."

"And because you enjoy adventure and anything that is a little beyond the humdrum of everyday life," she said.

"Oh no," he said. "Those are your own reasons, you wanton harridan."

She shrugged.

**

"Ah. Rosedene," Jack said, looking at the name etched into the stone pillar at the bottom of the driveway.

"Thank you so much for assisting with this." She had grown serious as they approached the house. Now it was the dark of early evening, and the street lamps were few out in the suburbs.

"Not at all. When we are done here – well, when my part is done – I shall be back in town in time for the first hand of cards at my club."

She passed him the key that she had been given by Inspector Gladstone. "If we both count to one hundred, that should give me enough time to get into my place before you begin."

"Yes. Well, go then."

She slipped away around the side of the house. It was almost fully dark here and the starlight did not penetrate the overhanging trees but she kept her hand outstretched and touching the dark bulk of the house, and she had been this way before anyway. She reached the shadowy crevice that contained the door that had been left open on her previous visit.

She waited, still counting, until she reached one hundred. Then she waited a little longer. Jack would be unlocking the door with great flamboyance and noise, and walking into the hall about now. If Mrs Newman was hiding in the house, this would attract her attention. Meanwhile, it was now time for Marianne to slip into the house via the back way.

She bent and unlaced her boots, and held them in her hands as she tiptoed along the freezing cold floor. If she was going to make a habit of creeping around houses, she'd have to invest in some silent shoes. Maybe overshoes made of felt? She filed that idea away for later. She reached the large central hallway and stopped, hiding herself behind the door that opened out in the vast space.

Jack was still there, calling out, "Hello? Is anybody here? Oh, bother." He gave an exaggerated sigh and walked out, making each footfall deliberate and heavy. The door was locked again behind him. He had not wanted to be stuck on the outside while she did what she had to do, but it was the only way to draw Mrs Newman's attention away.

Marianne hoped that this distraction had been enough. Without it, she had run the risk of encountering Mrs Newman unexpectedly. But with Mrs Newman's attention bent on Jack, she would not have noticed Marianne also slipping in.

What she should do next was still unclear. Marianne tried to put herself in Mrs Newman's shoes. What would she be likely to do now? If she thought that she was alone once more, she would go about her business.

The more urgent question was this: exactly what *was* her business?

So Marianne waited in the darkness, listening so hard that

the sound of her own heartbeat threatened to overwhelm her.

She went rigid. She heard footsteps, slow and measured, passing overhead, just thuds on the carpeting. Then the walker had moved onto wooden floors and their boots sounded louder as they went to the uninhabited wing of the house. A door opened and closed.

Marianne waited but the door did not sound again and the house was utterly silent.

She couldn't stay where she was any longer. She took a deep breath and crept up the stairs, but she did not follow the direction of the footsteps. Instead she turned to the left and headed for the Grand Bedroom once again. She entered as noiselessly as she could, and was pleased to find that the curtains were open. Enough light was coming from the stars and the moon from this angle, to cast the room in shades of grey. She could make out the furniture and the general layout.

She slipped over to the bed and put the box on the floor. It fitted with just a few eighths of an inch to spare. Carefully she attached the long grooved strip, arranged the magnet, and pushed it deep underneath the bed. It could just be detected if you curled your fingers up and under the edge of the bed.

She knew that she should now leave, immediately. But she remembered what Simeon had said previously: the phonograph, or whatever was causing the noise, did not have to look like a phonograph. While she was here, then, she could not resist searching again. She began a fresh fingertip search of the place with one particular aim: this time, she was looking for anything that might be some *part* of a phonograph.

She examined the lamp on the dresser. She pressed every inch of the dresser itself. She peered behind chairs, under chairs, and worked her way right over, under and along the magnificent four-poster bed.

It had carvings in the massive posts, and the bed base seemed solid but as she went, using her fingers as much as her eyes, something moved. Her heart nearly stopped. She worked at the hidden drawer hastily and it slid out after much prodding.

It was empty.

It was not large enough to hide anything like a phonograph, and if some noise-making device had been hidden in there, how had it been operated and how had the noise escaped from the drawer? It was a dead end. Except that now she was certain where the jewellery had originally been hidden. She pushed the drawer closed again and continued on her search.

It was fruitless. She went to the corridor and listened hard, but Mrs Newman had not come out from her hiding place. Marianne went across to the room opposite to the Grand Bedroom and resumed her search. She had to pull the drapes back from the window, and when she turned to face the room, she had a little jolt of fear until she recognised the pale, grinning face as nothing but a child's doll. She'd noticed it before.

There was something horrible in its blank eyes and the mouth was half-open like it was singing. It was a female doll, in layers of lace and satin, and was propped up against the wall, facing the door. She tried to recall where it was the last time she'd seen it. Had it been moved? Other toys remained on the table.

She picked it up and found that it was heavy, with a solid

body and articulated arms and legs. As she moved it, something clicked, just like last time. She had thought it was its mechanism but now she began to ask herself – *what* mechanism, exactly?

She turned the doll over and looked at its back. There was a handle protruding out of it. Intrigued, she carried it to the window to make the most of the moonlight, and unlaced its frilly dress. The metal body had a spiral of holes in the front.

She turned the handle at the back, just a few revolutions, and stopped in horror as an unearthly noise began to come from the sound hole in the chest. She pressed it to her skirts to muffle the screeching. She could hear in the tones that once, it had indeed recited a nursery rhyme. As the sounds died away, she turned the doll over again, and looked at the mechanism in its back. There was the wax cylinder but it was pitted and degraded now. No wonder it had descended into terrifying noises.

This was the source of all the anguish. She still didn't know why, but at least she had the how – and it certainly didn't involve ghosts. She rearranged the doll's clothing to something more seemly, and headed for the door.

She opened it quietly, stepped through, and then it all went black with a bang.

Twenty-four

She came around slowly, as if she were swimming to consciousness out of a dream, becoming aware of her surroundings bit by bit. She didn't move. She was lying on a wooden floor, and there was a cruel cold draught by her hand. Her head throbbed. She opened her eyes slightly and saw nothing, making her panic at first, until she realised that it was still night.

She was still upstairs, in the passage between the Grand Bedroom and the room where she had found the doll. She listened carefully but could hear nothing. She wriggled just enough so that she could reach a hand to the top of her head, just above her temple, where she had received the blow, and there was already a lump forming. Her skin was hot to the touch.

She sat up. She didn't know how long she had been unconscious for. Probably not long, or Jack would have battered the place down by now. She was apparently alone, but who knew if Mrs Newman was watching from a crack or a hole somewhere. And perhaps others, too. There was no sign of the singing doll. She got to her feet, steadying herself against the door frame as her vision blurred and her head swam. Her newly-purchased bonnet remained on the floor and she didn't think she could bend to pick it up without swooning. She'd go home hatless; it was a good job she was not returning to Woodfurlong. Mrs Davenport would have had even more to berate her about.

As for Rosedene, her cover had been completely blown.

She still assumed it was Mrs Newman hiding in the house, and now she could assume that Mrs Newman was also behind the doll's screaming, or why else would she have taken it from Marianne? It was evidence.

She couldn't even begin to grasp *why* any of this might have happened.

But Mrs Newman had blown her own cover, too. Until that point, she must have realised that Marianne could not tell for sure if the house was unoccupied. Now it was obvious that someone else was there.

Marianne had to move fast and get to the police station. But moving fast was difficult, and made pains stab in her head, and she inched her way down the stairs. She rescued her bag from where she had hidden it in the kitchen, and let herself out of the back scullery door.

Jack was waiting for her on the street outside, leaning against a tree and smoking. He grinned and waved as he saw her. "All sorted? Well done, you. How did – oh my God, Marianne, what in blazes have you done?"

"Does it look bad?"

"It makes me wince to see it. Come here. Is your skull cracked?"

"Can you see my brains?"

"No. Perhaps you don't have any. That would account for all of this. But I can see your hair, and there is blood in it, and it is matted and they will not let you into a cab in this state."

"I can walk," she said weakly. "I was hit on the head. But it doesn't matter."

"It matters!"

"No, well yes, but listen. I know how the screaming was created, and it proves someone else was in the house. I should tell Inspector Gladstone at once."

"You should be attended to by a doctor at once. Anyway, the Inspector will be at home now, like a normal person. Oh, this is going to cost me money. Come here, Marianne." He put an arm around her, and she sank into his weight immediately. He held her up with the rough practicality of a soldier carrying a fellow through a battlefield, without ceremony or attention, and half-dragged her along the street until they found a late-night cabbie who could be persuaded – with enough money – to ignore the head injury and strange state of Marianne, and drive them to the police station.

Jack wouldn't let her sleep again. Every time she drifted off, he jabbed her or spoke sharply to her, keeping her awake until they rolled up to the police stationhouse. Inspector Gladstone was known to work late and start early, but he was hardly at work in the small hours. Luckily another constable recognised her. They were admitted, and by the time that the Inspector came in to work before dawn a few hours later, she had been cleaned up, examined, and plied with food and drink and medicine. There was a matron employed at the station, one of a new breed of severe spinster women concerned with morality and good manners, who attended to the women and children. She dealt with Marianne with the same brusque manner that she would deal with prostitutes and runaways. But she was not cruel, and she had even found a partly-decent bonnet for Marianne to wear.

Jack had long since disappeared. He said he still had the card game to attend, but she knew it was a lie; he had missed it by many hours. He just didn't want to be around the police, much like Simeon though for different reasons.

When Inspector Gladstone saw her, he commented on her bonnet at once. "Miss Starr. Interesting headwear. My grandmother wears just the same."

"I cleave to an older, more honest style," she replied, patting the deep bonnet that effectively shielded her face like a pair of blinkers for a horse.

He laughed and then grew serious. "They tell me you have been violently assaulted."

"That's a dramatic description. I have been whacked on the head and left unconscious, and robbed."

"Robbed?"

"Well, not exactly. I returned to Rosedene last night, and during the course of the evening I have discovered the source of the noise. I was bringing you the offending instrument when I was struck a blow on the head and knocked unconscious. When I came to, the article had been taken." She described the doll and how she thought it had worked. "So you see, the place is not empty and I know it is Mrs Newman who hides there still."

The Inspector listened carefully. "This is, indeed, worrying. I just wish I knew why she has gone to all these lengths – especially now, when the will is done with and all is settled. What more can she hope to gain?" he asked.

Marianne laughed. "I can help you answer that, sir. There is a set of jewels that has been hidden in that house, and she knows of their existence, and she has been trying to discover their secret hiding place."

"And you are going to tell me you know where they are?"

"Yes. They are in a box under the bed in the Grand Bedroom, and I know it for certain, as I put them there last night."

Inspector Gladstone rubbed his temples. "You will have to start at the beginning, and I fear we will need coffee."

She outlined how she had discovered the existence of the jewellery through Tobias, and proceeded straight to the plans for a séance. Gladstone interrupted her.

"How did you persuade the auction house to let you borrow them for this little escapade?"

"Ahh." She smiled nervously. "They are, as yet, unaware of their role in this."

Gladstone put his head in his hands. "I need to arrest you."

"I've admitted to nothing."

"You have. You have literally just told me…"

"What? Nothing. You have plenty of other things to worry about, Inspector. Now, we need to prise Mrs Newman out of her hiding place, am I not correct?"

"Yes. But how? Do we burn the house down?"

"We've dismissed that idea. A woman cannot hide in a house forever!" Marianne said. "What about a priest hole? She must be in a priest hole. It is an old house. Now, you could return with measuring rules and string and chalk and make a note of all the dimensions of each of the rooms. Somewhere, she will be hidden, in a secret cubby hole. But this will take a great deal of time, and she can evade you, sneaking from place to place. Tobias told us that. So I have devised another way. We will hold a séance and contact the ghost of poor Miss Dorothea. She will tell us where the jewels are."

"But you already know where they are. *And* you don't believe in ghosts."

"No, but Mrs Newman does; she has tried to pretend not to, but that is her underlying belief. And when the fake Miss Dorothea reveals the hiding place to us, you can bet that Mrs Newman will be listening. She will go immediately to the place and she will be caught red-handed. Do you see?"

"She will not believe that you are involved in such a scheme."

"Perhaps not. But she will believe that *you* are."

"No. I cannot." Gladstone was shaking his head vehemently. "There is absolutely no way that I can be involved in these shenanigans."

"We need a figure of authority from the police," she insisted. "As you say, she will not believe me, and I shall play the part of a sceptic the whole way through. Well, I shall simply be myself. But if an official presence is there, we are given a veneer of respectability."

"You can have Constable Bolton."

"He is hardly a figure of authority."

"He wears the uniform and quite frankly, Miss Starr, it is more than I ought to offer you."

"Thank you," she managed to say with grace. She started to get to her feet. "It happens tonight. There is still much planning to be done. Is Constable Bolton on duty? I will speak to him."

"Not right now, you won't. Sit back down. I will call for someone to take you home."

"That won't be necessary. Anyway, I am ... lodging ... with my friend."

"You have been injured in the line of duty. It is the least I can do. And by 'friend', I assume you're with that moon-touched lad, Simeon Stainwright. We know where he lives, don't you forget. Just tell me, before you go, where you want Bolton to be, and when."

***

Simeon was appalled by her state and she allowed herself to be led to the bed where she collapsed onto it. Her eyes felt gritty and dry, and her throat ached. Her head was throbbing. The doctor at the police station had given her a little bottle which smelled acrid and brown, and she took another two drops of it on her tongue. There was a hint of opium in it, and who knew what else, but it took the edge off the pain. She lay flat on her back, as lying on her side in her corsets was not comfortable. And she drifted away while Simeon clattered and scraped and knocked and banged and thumped away with tools and wood in the other room.

She woke to voices. She picked out Jack's low rumble, and his occasional laugh. There was Phoebe, speaking in a rapid and high tone, which suggested her excitement or perhaps her fear. And another laughing male voice, which she realised was Constable Bolton.

So, she thought. It is time. I wonder if we can really pull this mad scheme off?

She sat up slowly, feeling creased and crumpled. Her hair was a tangled mess at the back, but the wound had not opened up again, which was a blessing. As she moved slowly around the room, trying to find her hairbrush, Phoebe tapped on the partly-open door and came in.

"Oh, sit down," Phoebe said. "You look like you've fought a rose bush, and lost terribly."

Marianne sat, as ordered, and Phoebe produced a comb from her bag and set about arranging her hair.

"Are we doing the right thing?" Marianne asked.

"Of course not. It is ludicrous, every bit of it," Phoebe said. "But isn't it delicious? One day we shall be dead, Marianne. I do not know about you, but I intend to fill every moment with life and action. Not much is open to me beyond wife and mother, and I don't mind; I adore my life. But that is no reason for me to turn down the chance to fill it with a little more than housekeeping records and dinner party gossip."

"I wish I had your lightness of character," Marianne said, wincing as Phoebe tugged knot after knot out of her hair. "There must be an easier way to get Mrs Newman out of that place. I suggested to Inspector Gladstone they measure every room."

"How long will that take?"

"I don't know. A day?"

"Then it's an option, isn't it? But this Mrs Newman, she already knows you are on to her, because she has taken that doll and battered you on the head – don't worry, Simeon told me everything, and it sounds most thrilling. So she will be actively avoiding you. If you flood the place with police, she will simply hide, or flee."

"That would be good. If she flees, she will be caught."

"Definitely?" Phoebe asked. "How many police would you have to surround the place, to ensure she could not slip away unnoticed?"

"Rather a lot," Marianne said. "But it is not impossible. I doubt there is a secret tunnel from the place." Even as she said it, she worried that there might be.

"And how many police has the Inspector given you?"

"One. Bolton."

"There you are then. Not enough for all the windows and doors."

"Phoebe, are you actively encouraging me to simply dive headlong into the séance idea?"

"Yes, of course I am. I am your bad angel, sitting on your shoulder, urging you to be more daring. It might go terribly wrong, but what a hoot if you succeed!"

"You wish only to live vicariously through me."

"Indeed so. Now, let us bundle up your hair out of the way.

We can cover the worst of that bruise on your forehead easily. There. Now, you smell a little but I have some fragranced water with me. Let me spray your clothes and put a little powder on your face, and you are almost fit to be seen."

Marianne submitted to the ministrations and sighed. There were easier ways to get Mrs Newman out of the house – measuring and tearing down walls, burning it to the ground, surrounding it with men that they did not have – but they had opted for the most non-destructive way, and that was that.

Twenty-five

They trooped into Rosedene through the front door, without a hint of secrecy about it. Constable Bolton had surprised Marianne by agreeing to his role instantly and with a certain amount of relish. As long as she told him exactly what to do, so that he need make no effort in having to think for himself, he was perfectly happy. Jack had rolled his eyes dramatically, and made a variety of sensible objections, but ultimately he, too, had accepted his suggested role. Phoebe seized upon her role with pure enthusiasm, of course. Simeon was quiet, watching and listening, too afraid to take on any particular character. Much like his stage presence, he appeared wooden and nervous. But that was going to be all right; it made sense to him, in the context of what they were pretending to do, after all. He was the one tasked with carrying the talking board.

And Marianne quashed her worries and her fears, and decided that now was the time to simply act.

Jack, after his earlier faked cynicism, dived straight into his assigned character. He was to be a "scientist" of the paranormal, styling himself as a professor of the world of the spirit and mind, and he affected a booming, arrogant voice as he prowled around the large hallway as if for the first time.

"Oh, yes!" he declared. "I can feel a spirit here, for certain! What history! It is impossible, I tell you, simply impossible, for no mark to be left here. All the generations that have lived and died here have indelibly left their psychic imprints in the fabric of this building. Mark my words, Miss Starr, you shall have your preconceptions shattered. Quite shattered!"

Phoebe was reprising her role as the medium. It was far more accepted, in these circles, that a woman be the conduit for the "lost souls" to speak through – only a few men had made mediumship their speciality. Women were thought to be closer to the "other side" and more in touch with vague emotions, and far less likely to upset things by virtue of masculine rational thought and other manly occupations. Women, in their natural state of passivity, could simply let the words of the ghosts flow through them. A man, being more active and intelligent, would seek to control or interpret what was happening, and would thus disrupt the flow.

Marianne could scoff all she liked at those ideas, but it was what everyone said that they believed, and so she had to follow suit. And Phoebe was happy to be able to indulge in her theatrical fantasies. She was decked out in furs, and wore a hat that was a startling shade of red with half a peacock emerging from the top of it, in an eye-watering clash of colours. Phoebe followed Jack's lead, and stood in the centre of the dingy, dark hall, inhaling deeply with her eyes closed. "Oh, yes, I can already feel the promptings of the spirit."

"Utter nonsense," Marianne barked. At least she didn't have to feign or hide her own true feelings. "You can probably feel a chill from an open door, and maybe a hint of mould in the air. There is nothing here but a dead house. Whoever hit me on the head will be long gone, I am sure of it."

"Don't be so sure, miss," Constable Bolton said, stepping into his role. "Inspector Gladstone is a very modern man and he insists we explore all the avenues open to us. Something is still happening here, and we will get to the bottom of it."

"Passing housebreakers, nothing more," she snapped.

"The spirits of the past are thrumming in the air!" Phoebe warbled. "They have messages for us!"

Marianne sighed. "This is a nonsense and a charade. But come along, then. I am exceedingly interested to watch this experiment fail, as it must – as they all must."

They bickered their way up the main staircase. Only Simeon remained silent. At the top, Marianne made as if to turn left, along to the wing of the house that had previously been inhabited.

"No," Phoebe breathed, with her arms flung out dramatically. "I am called to this corridor." She pointed along the empty, mothballed passage.

"I have been here before," Marianne said, loudly. "That section has not been used for many years. See, this simply proves what bunkum this is. If you truly felt prompted by the spirits, you would have come this way, towards the Grand Bedroom."

"No," Phoebe said, swaying in an apparent rapture. "We must seek out a small room that was once very dear to a small child, decades ago. I am hearing a name … Dolly? Dottie? Come! Follow me! I am being led."

Jack said, "I believe her. It is well known that when a person dies, their ghost will often revert to the form in which the person was most happy. For many people, this would be when they were a child, you see."

He was making it up on the spot. But it sounded good enough, and Marianne trudged along behind, demonstrating unwillingness with every step. Constable Bolton burbled his way next to Simeon.

Phoebe pressed her hands to the third door along. Marianne had recalled that there had been a circular table in there, under a white sheet, and instructed Phoebe accordingly. She flung the door open and said, "Yes! Here is where she played as a child, and here we can speak once more to her. In we go, in we go! Yes, yes."

They left the door to the corridor standing open.

Jack fussed with a lamp that he had brought with him, and lit it, placing it on the floor by the open door. Simeon started to arrange chairs around the table, while Phoebe directed Constable Bolton to remove the dust sheet from the table. The room was gloomy. The last of the light was fading from outside, and the dirty windows reflected the weak lamplight back at them. Their shadows loomed up large on the walls like a hideous puppet show.

Phoebe told them where to sit. Marianne was placed so that she had her back to the door. Constable Bolton was opposite her. Jack and Simeon made up the quarters of a circle, and

Phoebe began to act as if she were distressed.

"An uneven number, how foolish of me, how silly."

Marianne got to her feet. "I'll leave."

Phoebe pushed her back down. "No. Tonight, we will change your mind, forever! I am sure the spirits will forgive us this asymmetry." She took the spare chair in between Constable Bolton and Marianne, and they all placed their hands flat on the table-top, linking their fingers.

They placed the talking board in the centre of the table. The rectangular piece of wood was painted with all the letters of the alphabet, and a few extra phrases around the outside – yes, no, good evening and good night. Simeon had made a small wheeled table that rolled freely over the board. It was a design based on the older planchette, which had a pencil attached to it, but was simpler to use.

Everyone seemed to be treating the whole affair so lightly, but Marianne was feeling stressed. She had to make an effort to stop her brain running constantly over all the things that could go wrong. Be a stoic, she told herself. There is nothing I can do except respond to what is happening in the present moment. She forced her breathing to slow down, and focused on an awareness of the tension in her body, identifying the spots of knotted muscle, and consciously relaxing them.

Silence cloaked them now.

The lamp was turned down as low as possible. Marianne had not closed her eyes but she could see that everyone else had. Even Constable Bolton, who really ought not to be getting quite so much into the part. She narrowed her eyes, in case Mrs

Newman was watching from some secret corner. But then, Mrs Newman, if she were to be watching, knew that Marianne was a sceptic and could therefore assume that Marianne would be likely to be keeping her own eyes open, watching for tricks.

Phoebe began to call for the help of the spirits, according to the script that they had worked out earlier.

"Miss Dorothea Newman, we are calling on you to come to our aid, and the aid of the Metropolitan Police."

Then there was another long pause.

The sentence was designed to lure Mrs Newman in. If she truly believed in spirits, she would not be able to ignore the possibility that Miss Dorothea would indeed manifest herself. And what would she reveal? Would she tell everyone the name of her murderer? Mrs Newman would have to stay and listen, just in case.

Marianne started to think about Macbeth. It would be awfully handy for the actual ghost of Miss Dorothea to pop up and point directly at Mrs Newman's hiding place. Oh, if only!

Phoebe repeated her call twice more. They all placed their index fingers on the rolling table and let it begin to move. It really did feel as if it was moving of its own accord but they were all letting it rumble over to "good evening."

Phoebe gasped. "The spirit has arrived!" Then she let her head roll forwards, her chin onto her chest, and she moaned in a long and rather effectively chilling way. Even Marianne's hairs stood up on the back of her neck. Phoebe jerked her head upright suddenly and when she spoke again, it was in the high-pitched tone of an older woman, edged with rough gravel, cracking and modulating from tinny to hoarse and back again. It was close enough to how Miss Dorothea had spoken, and any variance would be explained by the fact that she literally didn't have a corporeal presence any longer.

"Who disturbs my sleep?" Phoebe warbled as Miss Dorothea.

Without hesitation, Jack spoke. "I am Professor Albert Edgeworth. We apologise for intruding on your time. Please, Miss Dorothea, can you tell us where you are? Can you speak? You may spell out your answers if you prefer."

It was not really what they wanted to know, but it was a necessary part of the deception. What else would a paranormal researcher ask, after all? And the talking board was nothing but a prop. The fake spirit *had* to speak.

"I am surrounded by light," Phoebe said. Marianne had given her various things to read; accounts by other mediums and supposed eyewitnesses. "Everything is faint and blurry. I do not think I will tarry here long. There is a journey I must make. That we all must make…" She let her voice fade away.

Constable Bolton made his move. "How did you die, miss?"

"Oh … oh …" Phoebe whispered. Marianne kicked her under the table, trying to remind her to speak up so that Mrs Newman could hear her properly. "Oh! It is a blur. I was asleep and then there was a … a darkness … something pressed down upon me, and then, I was floating … floating away."

"Humph. Well, thank you," he said.

Marianne spoke for the first time. She made her voice bored and flat. "Very well, I shall play along. We're looking for something, Miss Dorothea. Something hidden and no-one knows where it is. We know it exists because we have spoken with a boy that you were close to."

"What is it that you seek?" Phoebe asked.

"Ah, you see, I am not playing that game," Marianne said. "It would be too easy for you to cheat."

Jack said, sharply, "The spirits do not cheat! If you accuse them of lying, they will leave."

"Fine, fine. I am sorry. Miss Dorothea, there is a set of jewels that have been passed down the Newman family line, to the firstborn on their marriage."

"The necklace, the earrings, the bracelets and the brooch," Phoebe said, sounding joyous. "Oh, yes! Such things of beauty. Ah, the brooch – you have never seen an emerald so large!"

"Good God," Bolton said. "How could she possibly know all that, if she is a fake and a cheat? Miss Starr, I think you must consider your mind to be changed."

Marianne said, "Even this might have been faked. Such jewels do not pass down the generations without some remark or notice. A good medium speaks to everyone that she can before a séance, and discovers all these secrets in advance."

"Then tell us, Miss Dorothea, where these priceless items are hidden," Jack instructed.

Phoebe let a sly note enter her voice. "And why should I?"

"They need to go to the next generation," Constable Bolton said with confidence and authority. Marianne was profoundly grateful to the man. He seemed to be enjoying himself very much. "This house is to be sold and then where will they be? Ought they not stay in the Newman line?"

"Yes. Yes…"

"Are they in the house?" Marianne asked.

"Yes." Abruptly the talking board indicated "yes" too, the little table trundling decisively across the letters. Marianne wondered who was moving it, and why they were bothering. They are hidden, hidden low, in a place of sanctity."

"A chapel?"

"No, no! The heart of peace and repose. Hidden there for Cecil to claim them as he always should have done. His mother wanted him to have them."

"But Cecil Newman is dead."

"And so they rest in the place that he used to play as a child."

"A playroom, or a nursery," Marianne said. "How tediously obvious."

"You are clouded by your own sense of intelligence, woman."

Marianne bristled even though this was all in jest.

Phoebe continued. "As a child, sitting on the floor, where small spaces become large and the legs of tables are become forests and new lands can be found beneath cloths and in drawers."

"Definitely a nursery," Marianne said.

"Or a schoolroom," Jack suggested.

Phoebe laughed. The talking board rumbled and indicated "no."

"He was not an only child, but he did not want to play with his siblings. Nurseries and schoolrooms were not his haunt. Only me. He stayed with *me*. He was ever my favourite child…"

"What does that mean?"

"Go there. To our place of sanctity. You need to press upwards. First, bend down and then with your fingers press upwards and then it will slide right out at you…" Phoebe's voice grew fainter again. "The light is growing stronger and I feel that they are calling me. I always loved him, Cecil. He was ever my favourite child and such a comfort…" The final words were nothing more than a breath.

Phoebe shuddered and slumped forward. The wheeled table rolled over to "good night" and stayed there.

Constable Bolton jumped to his feet. "Water for the lady! She has fainted!"

"And then we must go and find this nursery," Jack said.

"I don't think that she meant that," Marianne replied. "She said that was not his haunt. Something closer to Miss Dorothea."

"Oh, so you do now believe her?"

"Ha." Marianne went towards the door and listened hard. Somewhere, a door clicked closed, quietly. So Mrs Newman had taken the bait. Hopefully she would understand that "Miss Dorothea" was urging them to the Grand Bedroom once again. After all, she had always suspected the jewels were hidden there. Now she had the clearer instructions to bend down and press upwards, and she was not a stupid woman. Hopefully she would soon find the hidden box – and be trapped by the snare activated by the removal of the jewellery.

"Has she gone?" Simeon whispered. He was the only person still sitting at the table, frozen in anxiety.

"I think so. Come on. We need to catch her. Constable, this will need you at the forefront."

He sprang into action. He could walk remarkably quietly and everyone else followed him, with Marianne being closest at his heel. They padded along the corridor and across the carpeted landing area, and into the inhabited wing. Jack came at the rear with the lamp, shielding it from cold draughts as they passed across the staircase in case the glass cracked.

The door to the Grand Bedroom was open. It was the only open door along the passageway. A yellow light spilled out and they could hear noises from within; a scraping sound, like wood on wood, and then a click and a thump.

Constable Bolton sprang to the door and Marianne elbowed her way in after him.

Mrs Newman was kneeling on the far side of the great wooden bed, and only the top of her head could be seen as she bent over the box that she had managed to find. She heard them enter but at the same time, her hand must have strayed into the box and they all heard the loud snap as the metal loop was triggered to snare around her wrist.

She screamed and jumped up, hugging the small box to her chest with her free arm, keeping her trapped hand between her body and the box. "Get away from me! This is mine, mine by rights!"

"Those belonged to Miss Dorothea and she has left them to Tobias."

"Well, that evil boy killed poor, sweet Miss Dorothea. And if she had really left them to him, why would they be here, hidden?"

"Because we put them there," Marianne said.

Mrs Newman cackled suddenly and didn't bother to reply. She spun around and ran for the door. The other door. The door that connected the Grand Bedroom to the anteroom that Constable Bolton and Marianne had set up their initial watch in.

"Get her!" Marianne screamed even as everyone leaped into action. Jack ran back out into the corridor while Constable Bolton pursued Mrs Newman into the anteroom. Marianne dithered only a moment, and then went after Constable Bolton, leaving Simeon and Phoebe to make up their own minds where to go.

That snare was supposed to shock her into not moving and cause her pain with every movement, Marianne thought. Damn it! An animal caught in a snare would endure endless torment and still try to escape. She should have remembered there were two exits to that bedroom, too. Constable Bolton showed a rare turn of speed and pursued Mrs Newman down the corridor.

"Don't let her out of your sight!" Marianne yelled. Jack overtook her, followed by Simeon. "Damn these skirts, damn them, damn them…" she muttered, struggling even to breath as her lungs threatened to explode out of her corset.

She slowed down. She would have to trust to the others, now.

Twenty-six

Phoebe caught her up. "Let the men catch her, as they surely will," she said. They gathered up their yards of heavy fabric and went down the stairs as quickly as they could with any safety. The main door was standing open. When they got to the steps outside, they stopped. Simeon was there, alone.

"Where have they all gone?"

"Jack and the policeman went off down the driveway."

"Could you see Mrs Newman?"

"I think she went ahead. But I thought I'd stay in case she doubled back."

"I don't imagine that she will return now. She's got what she wanted," Marianne said morosely. "I am such a bloody fool. That second door! And I spent a night in that room. I should have remembered. Now she has the jewellery and she can escape. Escape with money, and escape from justice." Her guilt made her feel physically sick as she went over and over her mistakes.

"No, listen to me," Phoebe said.

Marianne did not want to listen. She shook Phoebe's hand off her arm and walked down to the gravel driveway, heading around the bend of dark trees and towards the road.

"Wait," Phoebe said, more urgently. "You have saved Tobias, haven't you?"

"They need to hang someone and if they can't get her, they'll just hang him instead," Marianne said bitterly. She picked up her pace and as she rounded the last dark tree she saw three figures up ahead where the drive met the main road.

Why had they stopped?

She broke into a run.

Everything happened very quickly.

Jack was holding the lamp high with his arm outstretched but here, outside, it did not cast much light save for illuminating him. Constable Bolton was a smaller, rounder blob, shouting at the silhouette of Mrs Newman.

And she had stopped because of the cart blocking the way, and the man on the back of the cart who was standing up and yelling.

The air turned brilliantly, blindingly white, as if the sun had come to earth and exploded all around them. Marianne screamed and covered her face and she heard Phoebe cry out too. Yells erupted from Jack and Constable Bolton.

Mrs Newman wailed in sheer terror.

Marianne peeked through her hands. The light had gone and now all she could see was a white burning orb on the ground by the cart, which still burned with enough ferocity to light up the scene. Mrs Newman was on her knees, sobbing, and Constable Bolton had shot over to her. The figure on the back of the cart remained there, etched in a dramatic pose.

She knew that outline. With the solitary streetlamp behind him, and the light from the burning white stuff before him, it was clearly her father.

"My eyes," Phoebe whispered.

"Are you all right?"

"No; one eye hurts. I feel ill."

"Stay here. Simeon, stay with her."

"Gladly."

Marianne ran as fast as she was able. Her first point of attention was Mrs Newman, who was crying. "I am blind!"

"So is justice," said Constable Bolton, and then he laughed for ten seconds at his own joke as he prized the wire snare from around her wrist, and replaced it with his own set of handcuffs.

"I am not joking," she said. "I could not cover my eyes because of that box in my hand. I am blinded."

"I feel your pain," Jack said, coming towards them, with one eye squeezed shut. "I dropped the lamp. It's broken. What the hell happened? Did a star fall to earth?"

Russell Starr laughed at them all. "Marianne, dear daughter, I expect you can identify it."

It was a challenge that she had to accept. She stepped forward and examined the remnants of the burning white lump. It faded away. "Magnesium powder," she said. "But why on earth...? And father, why are you here?"

"They were sedating me. I will not stand for it, Marianne. I will not. I will not be treated like a wild dog. I pretended to take the stuff and spat it out into a potted plant when Mrs Crouch's back was turned. Then I grabbed my medicine and this boy here, and here I am." He poked the back of the stable boy with his outstretched foot. The lad grinned, enjoying every moment of his wild adventure.

"But what about the magnesium?"

"That's the thing," Russell said. "I have been experimenting with some new powders to pep me up a little. When I get tired, I can barely move. The druggist recommended some new stuff to take by mouth, and I bought a bag of it, and brought it home and put it down – and forgot where I put it. Or, more likely, it was tidied away by one of you busybodies."

"I did no such thing, but go on."

"I thought I might not be up to a night-time drive without some stimulant," he said. "I saw the bag on the bench as I passed through the laboratory and snatched it up, and as we drove here, I opened the bag to partake of the powder before we arrived. Alas, the first taste of it told me of my error."

"Oh! I found it behind the curtains and I moved it," she said, suddenly.

Jack had to interrupt. "Well, so now I want to know why you are storing bags of magnesium on windowsills."

"It's actually jolly useful for a range of things," he said. "When mixed with sulphur, I can create my own Epsom Salts at a fraction of the price and it is awfully good at restoring a certain regularity to one's daily habits."

"And on the windowsill?"

"I've already told you that I live with busybodies who like to 'help' by tidying things up. Anyway, not to worry. It wasn't what I thought it might be, but hasn't it proved jolly useful?

Boom! Ha, ha. Constable! Shall we drive that miscreant to the station?"

"That would be most useful, yes sir. Let us get the lady onto the cart."

Mrs Newman fought and screamed every step of the way as Jack, Constable Bolton and even Simeon had to lift her up and tumble her into the cart. Constable Bolton was more than happy to sit on her legs, and Jack kept hold of her arms. She resorted to spitting, and everyone moved to be out of range.

"Dear me, you are quite vile," Phoebe remarked and took a place next to the stable boy on the bench at the front of the cart.

The box had been passed back to Marianne. She sat at the far end, cradling the box and jewellery in her lap, and tried to process everything that had just happened as they rolled their way back into London.

As they pulled up at the police station, which was a raucous and noisy place at this time of night, Marianne spoke. Mrs Newman had, by this point, lapsed into a sullen silence.

"There really is no point in denying any of this, now, you know."

"Shut up. Don't speak to me."

"I am sorry for the loss of your husband and the ill-treatment that you feel you have had. I've read about how your husband's parents did not approve of the match, and that can't have been easy."

"What would you know, you dried up, vinegary old spinster?"

Jack laughed. "Oh, haven't you heard? We are engaged to

263

be married, you know."

Mrs Newman sneered and turned her head away. Which was good, because there was less likelihood of more spitting.

Constable Bolton went into the station and returned with enough policemen to carry Mrs Newman into the place without problem. Jack tipped his hat to Marianne and leaped down into the street. He bid her farewell and was immediately swallowed up by a passing rough crowd of men recently ejected from a public house. Marianne was about to get out of the cart herself but she saw the expression on her father's face.

"Married?" he blustered, hardly able to speak. "To that man? I thought it was a joke when I first heard it but…"

She was about to tell him that it was, but then thought of the deception with Mrs Davenport. "Don't worry. I will explain it all very soon."

Constable Bolton reappeared on the pavement and stretched out his hand. "Miss, you need to come inside and make statements, if you will."

"Marriage, Marianne? But I…" Russell was still saying as Marianne stepped out of the cart. She was followed by Phoebe and Simeon and he had to come along behind, still spluttering. One by one they were all taken into the stationhouse, and the boy with the cart was asked to drive home, and sworn to absolute secrecy, for the moment.

Twenty-seven

They were all separated instantly. Marianne and Phoebe were led away by the severe matron and put in small rooms, with the matron sitting in the doorway that joined them. Russell and Simeon went with Constable Bolton. Marianne had no choice but to make herself as comfortable as possible in the small, sparse room. She found that the wooden chair was impossible to relax upon. She alternated between pacing the empty room, and sitting, and looking at the matron, and sighing heavily.

She had to assume that Mrs Newman had been taken to some cells.

After what seemed like an interminably long time, they were given the chance to explain everything, and once their statements had been made, they were allowed home. Russell met them in the entrance, and revealed that he had enough money to pay for a cab to take them all the way home. Simeon darted off into the darkness before Marianne could speak with him.

"Father, I do not think I can come back to Woodfurlong."

"You can," Phoebe said. "You must."

"Damn right," Russell said. "I've had enough of pandering

to that woman."

"She is my mother."

"Everyone has a mother. But you don't get to choose them and you're under no obligation to like them."

"But it does say that we are to honour our father and mother," Phoebe protested as they climbed into the cab.

"Honouring is not the same as liking. Honour her all you like, but from a distance. God, I am tired. If anyone crosses me, I shall simply fall asleep on them, and pin them to the ground for twelve hours."

They had to laugh. Marianne was nervous about returning to Woodfurlong but she took comfort from her father's presence and Phoebe squeezed her hand. "It will all turn out for the best," she said.

And it did, but from a most unexpected quarter.

They rolled up the driveway in the small, dead hours of the night. London might teem with life at any hour, but the suburbs slumbered heavily. But the noise of the wheels and hooves on gravel brought someone to the front door. Mr Barrington had obviously been waiting for them. He looked tired but he broke into smiles as he ushered them all inside. The cabbie was paid and rumbled off.

"Shh," Phoebe said, putting her fingers to her lips.

"You will not wake the invalid. She has been dosed well," Mr Barrington said. "May I get you all some warm drinks or food from the kitchen?"

"How…?"

Mr Barrington grinned even more widely. "It is the warmest

room. If I might suggest you overlook the impropriety for one night, shall you all follow me there?"

So they did, because things were getting more strange by the moment. The kitchen's fire was out, but it held its warmth more readily than any other place. They crowded on the bench by the long table and Mr Barrington brought them some bread, pate, cheese and cold sausage. He also proved to be rather good at conjuring up a bottle of brandy.

"My mother will bury us all for this," Phoebe said.

Russell muttered something but no one could understand him, due to the mouthful of food.

"Where is Mrs Davenport?" Marianne asked, her suspicions rising. "Oh Phoebe. You did not go ahead and buy fly papers, did you?"

"I did not!"

Mr Barrington said, "No one need be alarmed, but Mrs Davenport has been taken ill this afternoon. She is sleeping deeply after the most helpful attentions of Mrs Crouch, who has kindly agreed to stay overnight to tend to her. I have already sent word to Mr Davenport who will arrive tomorrow ... well, in a few hours' time ... to take her home to recover."

Everyone went very still. Of course, the natural instinct was to whoop and celebrate but on the other hand, she was ill.

"What kind of ill?" Marianne asked.

"Some kind of gastric fever. It is a mystery. But Mrs Crouch assures us all that she will make a full recovery in time."

Marianne shot a look at her father, who was merrily drinking away, having gained his second wind in spite of the lack of stimulant powders. "Father, have you anything to say to this?"

"It is nothing of my doing! Speak to Mrs Crouch. She sees everything and hears everything, that woman. She's a gift. You mustn't be such a snob, Marianne. Everyone has their worth and I fear you might have overlooked hers."

"I am not a snob! But …" she tailed off.

"As long as my mother is in no real danger," Phoebe said, "then I, for one, am happy. It is time for bed. I should like to look slightly refreshed when my father arrives."

"You see," Russell said. "What a dutiful daughter and a credit to her father." He grinned at Marianne.

She sighed, and he winked, and they clinked their glasses together, and she thought that she might understand him, at last.

***

Marianne slept late and she didn't wake up until Emilia slipped into her room with a tray of food.

"I've missed having breakfast in bed," Marianne said, groggily, as she fought herself up and out of the bedsheets. Emilia fussed around the pillows so that Marianne could prop herself semi-upright. "How is Mrs Davenport this morning?"

"She appeared to be better but she was grateful to see her husband."

"Ah, he's here? I must dress…"

"No, no." Emilia poured some tea. "They have already left."

"Really?"

"Mr Davenport was anxious to take her home, and Mrs

Crouch was adamant that only her own bed and her own water would cure her. She said that she had learned, in the Crimea, of the way that a body adapts to the water and air of a local area, and that if you subjected yourself to unfamiliar water and air, you ran the risk of becoming ill. She said that this had happened to Mrs Davenport."

"Did she really? Well, well. And did Mrs Crouch administer any medicines?"

"Only a light tonic of her own preparation. She has been dosing Mrs Davenport for a number of days, apparently."

"Indeed." Marianne smiled. Mrs Crouch had access to their full laboratory, a wealth of medical knowledge, and a steely determination. They would never find out what was in the tonic. "And how is Phoebe?"

"Mrs Claverdon rose to greet her father when he arrived, and has retired once more to bed, and is currently in much the same state as yourself. Do you feel all right? I can ask Mrs Crouch for her tonic…"

"Ah, no, that will not be necessary. Thank you, Emilia. I imagine the whole household is breathing more easily now. What of Mrs Cogwell?"

"Unpacking as we speak."

"Then all is right with the world."

"It is, indeed."

Emilia withdrew, and Marianne picked at the eggs. For all was not right with the world, not yet – not while a young man remained in prison and set to hang for a murder that he did not commit.

***

But the wheels of the law ground slowly. Infuriatingly so. Marianne found the energy to go into London late that afternoon, though she moved with lead in her limbs. She was not able to speak to Inspector Gladstone. The constable at the desk said, "He is not your personal police officer, madam. I can help you with any enquiries that you might have."

He could not help. He would not tell her whether Tobias was still in custody, nor what was happening to Mrs Newman. Eventually, defeated, she went to see Simeon.

He was crouching on the floor, his bottom in the air, poking at a long thin wire that was coiled on the floorboards. He looked over his shoulder as she entered, and waved her in. "Ah, good to see you. Watch this." He touched a thin metal stick to the wire and from the other room came a shout of pain.

"Stop!"

"Oh." Simeon dropped the metal spike and sat back on his heels. "So it did not work, then?"

Tobias emerged. "No, it did not. That hurt. Oh! Miss Starr." He became immediately bashful.

"Tobias! Don't you get all shy with me, young man! I see you have been released."

"Yes. Thanks to you. I am not allowed to leave town. I am out on bail, they say. But the Inspector was pleased and said it was going to be all right. Simeon, I think we need to add more resistance."

"That will create more heat. I do not want my pants setting alight on stage."

"Why not? Could that not be part of the trick?"

"Oh – do you mean that we might fool the audience into thinking it had gone wrong…"

"Yes, exactly. Let me see how thick the wire is that you are using."

Tobias knelt down next to Simeon and both began to examine the appliance as if Marianne was not there.

She left them to it. She had the reassurance of knowing that Tobias was free, and the added bonus that Simeon was not alone.

She got home, and met her father in the hallway, who was demanding to know when she was getting married and did she really expect him to walk her down the aisle and if so, he would need a new hat.

She spent a long hour explaining the depths of her subterfuge to him. By the end of it, she was left with the impression that he was slightly disappointed that there was not going to be a big event. Ominously, he said, "Well, I shall have to look for my excitement elsewhere," and he took himself off to bed.

Marianne herself had a very early night.

Twenty-eight

Marianne was summoned to a meeting with Inspector Gladstone a full week later. She went into London a few hours earlier than the appointment, and took a detour.

Jack Monahan's housekeeper frowned at her.

"I believe that I am visiting within respectable hours now," Marianne said sweetly.

"Send her up!" Jack bellowed, who had obviously been listening or looking out of a window.

Marianne ascended the stairs and staved off any feelings of nervousness by plunging straight into the matter at hand. She held out some coins. "This is the money that I borrowed from you and forgot to pay back."

"Oh! That is the last thing I expected. Thank you, however." He took it from her and his hand brushed hers. She was glad that she was wearing gloves. She hastily put her hands behind her back, then felt too exposed like that, and folded them in front of herself instead.

"Thank you for all of your help," she said.

"You sound dreadfully formal. Are you about to present

me with a scroll and a golden watch as a token of your appreciation?"

"No, unless you would like such a thing."

"Not particularly."

"I have not forgotten what you would like," she told him. "I have been talking to Phoebe this week. We have a short list of eligible women who might take your fancy and we can begin to arrange the introductions – informally, at gatherings we will hold at Woodfurlong – as soon as you are ready."

He grimaced. "I regret ever mentioning it."

"With all seriousness, I will stop if it bothers you too much."

"It does bother me."

He turned away. She said, "I know what bothers you the most. It is the fact that you told me one honest thing about yourself, and now you feel vulnerable. Jack, this is not information that I intend to turn against you. It is not something I will use to bring you down or make you feel bad. If you want help in this matter, I will genuinely help you, and if you want me to drop it, I will do that too."

"But why?"

"Because I consider you a friend. And that is what friends do."

"Men and women cannot be friends."

"Oh, nonsense," she said, firmly. "We've actually done a jolly good job of it so far."

He didn't reply.

She sighed and moved back to the door. "Anyway, I shall leave it up to you. Simply send me a note, and Phoebe and I will spring into action. Until then, you may rest assured that I shall not bother you."

She had her hand on the doorknob when he turned back around to face her. He smiled, very slightly. "I don't mind you bothering me."

She smiled back, broadly. "Good. Now, I am off to see the Inspector, and let us hope this whole matter can be brought to an end."

***

"Has she confessed?" Marianne asked as soon as she was seated in front of Gladstone's desk.

"In a way. She shouts about this and that. She has certainly revealed many things to us, and proven your suppositions and guesses to be correct."

"They were not guesses! They were logic and reason."

"Well, however you came to your conclusions, you are exonerated. The notebook that Mr Stainwright gave us, with the jewellery we took from her possession, and the mechanical doll that we found hidden in the house this week, all back up your story. She has ranted and raved about what she believes to be her right, but the will is clear and legal; she inherits nothing."

"So she came back from America, and she was convinced that the Newman Set were hidden in the room that Miss Dorothea did not leave. She used the doll to scare her."

Inspector Gladstone nodded. "She brought the doll with her. It's one of Edison's things. I can see why they never took off, though. It is a horrible object to give to a child. She thought that Miss Dorothea would leave if she thought the house was haunted."

"But she didn't, so Mrs Newman needed another way to get into the room. Yet killing was not enough – she still couldn't find what she sought."

"She has confessed that her next plan of action was to pull up floorboards, rip down walls, and tear every scrap of furniture apart."

"She still would not have found the jewellery," Marianne said. "They were already at the auction house."

"Ah. Yes, about that," Gladstone said, and Marianne felt a little cold. He let her dangle for a few moments, and rearranged some of the paperwork on his desk while she waited.

"Sir, I…"

He laughed. "Miss Starr, the jewellery is back in the possession of Atticus, Purfoy and Atticus. They have asked me to thank you for exposing the flaw in their security system, and they will be upgrading to one of the newer devices within a month. They have also requested that once they have installed a new system, you are welcome to repeat your antics. They are curious to discover if their new system has flaws. You will be paid, of course."

"They are going to pay me to break in?"

"Quite so. Indeed, they have paid you for the last endeavour." Gladstone slid an envelope across to her. It contained a handful of guineas and she gasped. "A professional house-breaker, Miss Starr. It is a strange turn of career for a lady."

276

"No stranger than scientist," she said, pocketing the money before he could change his mind. "Although I do not intend to make a regular thing of it."

"So you return to your usual investigations?"

"I do. I have had two enquiries this week. My name has been spread over town lately, and I feared it would bring nothing but shame and ignominy. However, it seems that the general public is rather more forgiving than I had expected."

"Oh, you make a good story. You are larger than life, now, Miss Starr, and you can get away with more than the average woman on the street. That said, take care. For the public will turn in an instant and strike you down once they tire of you."

"That is a fear of mine. Thank you for the reminder," she said. "I shall ride the tide for as long as I am able, however."

"You might want to write your experiences for the press," he said. "Start cultivating a relationship with the journalists and get them on your side. That way, you can control, to some extent, how you are portrayed." He passed a small card over to her. "Start with this one."

To her shock, she saw that the name on the card was "Miss Adelia Digby."

"A woman? A woman who writes for the newspapers?"

"I thought she might be the most approachable and sympathetic. Also, she plagues me nearly as much as you do, wanting information and so on. I am throwing you to her as a sop."

"I see. I ought to be insulted."

"But you are not. Speak to her. You will benefit one another mutually." He got to his feet and Marianne rose. "The trial of Mrs Newman will be long and painful. In the meantime, will Tobias be safe with your friend?"

"I believe so."

"And your other friend … Mr Monahan? He flatly refuses to come to the station to make a statement."

"Please do not press him. Do you need him?"

"No. Not at this moment in time. But he is another useful fellow to know, isn't he?"

"He is, indeed," Marianne said.

Inspector Gladstone led her to the door and passed a second envelope to her as they left the room. "And these are your wages, as you have been working for us all along, in some capacity or another."

She started to look inside but he folded his hand over hers and prevented that. "Just take it. Travel in a first class carriage home for once."

"I need this money for my future."

"There is no such thing. There is only here and now. Enjoy something." He ushered her out into the crowded foyer and no more private conversation was possible. That was all right. They had said everything, and she didn't want to embarrass him with effusive gratitude. She was a professional, after all. She pushed both envelopes into her bag.

Constable Bolton waved to her, merrily, and nearly lost his grip on the drunken woman that he was escorting. Marianne waved back but he had already turned away to stop the woman biting another passing prisoner. Shouts erupted behind her. A policeman hailed Inspector Gladstone. She was surrounded by the daily chaos of a busy police station, and she left quickly.

The street outside was no more peaceful.

She stepped happily into the multitudes, and was swept away.

THE END

If you have enjoyed this book, please leave a review where you bought it!

If you have really, really enjoyed this book, why not sign up to my New Releases Newsletter? I don't share your email with anyone, and I don't spam. Here is the link to type into your browser:

http://www.subscribepage.com/o5y2q0

Made in the USA
San Bernardino, CA
02 May 2020